ABERDEEN
CITY LIBRARIES

Dominic took a deep breath and made his play. 'How would you feel about making the boss thing a more permanent arrangement?'

She wanted to say yes. It was a fantastic offer—something that would really let her build up her life as Faith Fowler. But how could she do it in the shadow of her family name? How could she risk living in London again, knowing that any moment the paparazzi could find her and thrust her back into the limelight?

Dominic gave her an encouraging smile and she tried to return it.

Would it really be so bad even if they did find her? She was a grown woman. And with a stable job with Dominic she'd never be reliant on her family for money or anything else again. This could be her chance at true independence.

Until Dominic found out the truth. There was no way he'd hang on to an employee who brought the paparazzi down on him for harbouring a missing heiress. And once they'd found her all the stories would start up again, the pictures of her leaving that damn hotel room would be back in circulation, and the rumours about her relationship with a married, drug addict rock star... No. Dominic wouldn't stand for any of that. Even if she could make him believe that the papers had it all wrong.

She couldn't stay. There was no place for her in Dominic's world any more—if there ever really had been. Getting close to Dominic... It was a mistake. One she was very afraid she might have already made. But there had to be a line, a point she couldn't cross. She couldn't fall in love. And so she couldn't risk staying.

Dear Reader

The idea for this book came to me a couple of years ago, around the time a lot of travel companies were folding and the news was filled with tourists stuck in airports, trying to find a way home. All of a sudden Faith strolled into my imagination, refusing to be beaten by a little thing like being unexpectedly jobless, broke and stranded in a foreign country.

I set most of Faith and Dominic's story in London—partly so I could relive my years as a conference and events planner, working in some of the capital's best hotels and venues. While I didn't get to experience all the things Faith does in the book, I certainly had plenty of adventures of my own! And the pelicans in St James's Park are my favourite things about the city, too.

But what I love most about this story is that it shows how far love can take you. It can make you do all sorts of things you never even imagined you could—let alone would want to! And above all love can make you the person you're meant to be.

I hope you enjoy Dominic and Faith's story—and the pelicans!

Love

Sophie x

HEIRESS
ON THE RUN

BY
SOPHIE PEMBROKE

Published in Great Britain 2014
by Mills & Boon, an imprint of Harlequin (UK) Limited,
Eton House, 18-24 Paradise Road, Richmond, Surrey, TW9 1SR

© 2014 Sophie Pembroke

ISBN: 978 0 263 24172 3

Harlequin (UK) Limited's policy is to use papers that are natural,
renewable and recyclable products and made from wood grown in
sustainable forests. The logging and manufacturing processes conform
to the legal environmental regulations of the country of origin.

Printed and bound in Great Britain
by CPI Antony Rowe, Chippenham, Wiltshire

Sophie Pembroke has been dreaming, reading and writing romance for years—ever since she first read *The Far Pavilions* under her desk in Chemistry class. She later stayed up all night devouring Mills & Boon® books as part of her English degree at Lancaster University, and promptly gave up any pretext of enjoying tragic novels. After all, what's the point of a book without a happy ending?

She loves to set her novels in the places where she has lived—from the wilds of the Welsh mountains to the genteel humour of an English country village, or the heat and tension of a London summer. She also has a tendency to make her characters kiss in castles.

Currently Sophie makes her home in Hertfordshire, with her scientist husband (who still shakes his head at the reading-in-Chemistry thing) and their four-year-old *Alice-in-Wonderland*-obsessed daughter. She writes her love stories in the study she begrudgingly shares with her husband, while drinking too much tea and eating homemade cakes. Or, when things are looking very bad for her heroes and heroines, white wine and dark chocolate.

Sophie keeps a blog at www.SophiePembroke.com, which should be about romance and writing but is usually about cake and castles instead.

Other titles by Sophie Pembroke:

STRANDED WITH THE TYCOON

For Mum & Dad
for always believing I could

CHAPTER ONE

'I DON'T UNDERSTAND,' Faith said, fingers gripping the fabric of her uniform too tightly. The body-hugging grey pencil skirt didn't have a lot of give, but she needed something solid and real in her hands. Something that definitely existed. Unlike the plane that was supposed to be taking her and her latest tour group back to London. 'How can there not be a plane?'

The airport official had the air of a man who'd had this conversation far more times than he'd like today, and in more languages than he was really comfortable with. It was in no way reassuring. 'There is no plane, *signorina*, because there is no company any longer. It's been declared bankrupt. All customers of the Roman Holiday Tour Company are being asked to contact their insurance companies and—'

'But I'm not a customer!' Faith interrupted, her patience exhausted. She'd been in the airport for three hours now, and she really needed a cup of coffee. Or an explanation for what the hell had happened to trash her immediate future overnight. 'I'm an employee. I'm the tour guide.'

The official's gaze turned pitying. Faith guessed that meant she wasn't likely to get paid this month. Or ever. Great. Just when her bank account could really have done with the help. 'Then I suggest you call your employer. If you are able to find him.'

Oh, that really didn't sound good.

Turning away, Faith gave what she hoped was a reassuring smile in the direction of the huddle of tourists waiting for her to report back on their journey home. Holding up her index finger in the universal 'just one minute' gesture, she fished in her capacious bag for her phone. Time to find out what the hell was going on.

'Marco?' she asked, the moment the phone stopped ringing. 'What the hell—'

There was a click on the other end of the line. *Thank you for calling the Roman Holiday Tour Company! There is no one available to take your call right now...*

Her own voice on the voicemail message.

Faith hung up.

Around her, Leonardo da Vinci Airport buzzed with life. The sounds of crackly announcements and suitcase wheels on smooth flooring. The chatter of excited holiday-goers. The smell of fast food and strong coffee. The twelve British tourists standing around their suitcases, looking at her hopefully.

Faith took a deep breath, and approached. 'Okay, guys, here's the situation. I'll be honest, it's not great, but I'm still here and I will help you sort everything out, okay?' Maybe she wasn't getting paid any more, and maybe her boss had disappeared off the face of the earth, but she'd spent the last two weeks showing these people the sights and sounds of Italy. They trusted her. She owed it to them to at least make sure they got home safely. Maybe, that way, their memories of this holiday wouldn't just be of a total disaster.

No one actually relaxed at her words, but at least they looked slightly less terrified, which Faith figured was the best she could hope for, given the circumstances. *Now for the hard bit.*

'So, let's start at the top. Does everybody have travel insurance?'

It took a full two and a half hours, four cups of coffee, twenty phone calls, and plenty of sweet-talking, but eventually Faith had everyone either rebooked on other flights or safely ensconced in a hotel room until their insurance could organise their return home.

Everyone, that was, except for her.

Dropping down to sit on one of the airport benches, ignoring the guy asleep with his head on his backpack next to her, Faith pulled out her phone and tried Marco's number again.

Thank you for calling the Roman Holiday Tour Company! There is no one available to take your call right now...

She jabbed the end call button, dropped her phone into her lap, and closed her eyes. Okay, so, time to review the situation. Where was she?

She was in Rome! Centre of history, romance and really great pizza. She knew her way around, she had, ooh, twenty euros in her purse, she...was unemployed, homeless and stuck.

Faith sighed, and opened her eyes again, looking around the busy terminal. Everybody there seemed to know exactly where they were going, and how they were going to get there. She didn't even know where she was going to sleep tonight.

She could call Antonio, she supposed. Except for the part where she really, really couldn't. Ex-boyfriends weren't generally inclined to be hugely helpful when her life fell apart, she'd learnt the hard way, and the one she'd left in a fit of anger only two weeks earlier would probably throw her out on her ear. Or worse.

And since everyone else she knew in Rome was either part of Antonio's ridiculously extended family or related to her missing employer, or both, that pretty much exhausted the local options.

Which left her with…home. She should be back in London by now, ready to pick up her next group and embark on a tour of the Italian lakes. She guessed that was off, too. She'd barely seen more of the homeland than the cheapest airport hotel at Heathrow since she left Britain a year and a half ago, and even if she hadn't cut all ties with the friends she'd had before that, how could she just call up and say, *Hey, I'm kinda stranded. Want to buy me a plane ticket?*

No, the only people anyone could do that to were family. And she really didn't want to have to call them, either.

She had no doubt that dear old Mum and Dad, the Lord and Lady Fowlmere, would welcome her back into the bosom of the family in no time. After all, the publicity of the wild child heiress returned to the Fowlmere estate would make great copy, and her father always loved anything that made him look good in the press.

Faith had left home three years ago, ready to be herself for once, not an aristocratic relic to be trotted out for charity galas and other occasions, or a standing joke in the society pages. Going home now would undo all that hard work. Not to mention bring up the reasons she'd had to leave in the first place.

But it didn't look like she had an awful lot of choice.

Rubbing a hand across her forehead, Faith straightened her white blouse, then ripped off the hideous orange and red necktie that Marco insisted on his guides wearing and shoved it in her bag. It meant that the neckline of her blouse was a little more revealing than was entirely appropriate, but she didn't care. If she was going to have to call her family, she needed a drink first. And perhaps flashing a little cleavage as she walked into the airport bar would mean that she didn't have to waste any of her precious twenty euros buying it herself.

'Explain to me again how this happened.' Lord Dominic Beresford looked at the icy-cold bottle of Italian beer sitting on the bar in front of him with longing. He'd spent all day in meetings, worked in the cab all the way to the airport, and was just ready to switch off and relax before his late-night flight back to London, when Kevin, the Temp from Hell, called.

Dominic's beer would have to wait until he'd fixed whatever Kevin had screwed up now.

On the other end of the phone line, he could hear Kevin frantically turning pages in one of the many files Dominic was sure he had stacked on his desk. Stupid Shelley and her stupid maternity leave anyway. Wasn't keeping him sane a higher calling than a baby?

Dominic swept a finger down the beads of water on the neck of his beer bottle. Even he had to admit, probably not.

'Um, best I can tell, sir, your secretary booked in the tour guide with your usual company some months ago. And then…' Kevin trailed off nervously.

And then, Dominic filled in mentally, the owner of that usual company, Lady Katarina Forrester, also known at the time as his fiancée, had been caught on camera in a rather compromising position, leading to a media storm that had threatened his family's reputation.

So he'd called off the engagement. And in retaliation she'd cancelled their professional relationship, too.

Which left him with six American businessmen and -women flying into London tonight, expecting entertainment and tourism to go with their meetings. And probably, now he thought about it, hotel rooms, too. Kat had always taken care of the accommodation for his business guests.

The fact that this was almost entirely his own fault for getting involved with a business contact in the first place didn't make Dominic want that beer any less. He should have known better.

'I think I can remember what happened next,' he told Kevin drily. 'But I'm more interested in what happens now. Here's what I need you to do. First—'

'Um…' Kevin said, the way he always did when he was about to ruin Dominic's day. Surely Shelley didn't need a full year off with the baby. What if she didn't come back at all?

'What?' Dominic bit out.

'The thing is, it's nearly eight o'clock, sir. I'm supposed to finish work at five-thirty.' Kevin sounded more whiny than apologetic about the fact. How had Shelley ever thought he'd be a fitting replacement for her? Unless her mothering instinct had kicked in early. Kevin certainly needed taking care of.

'Add the hours onto your time sheet,' Dominic said, attempting reason. 'I'll make sure you're compensated for your time.'

'Thank you, sir. Only it's not just that. I've got a… commitment tonight I can't break.'

'A date?' Dominic tried to imagine the lanky, spotty Kevin with an actual woman, and failed.

'No!' The squeak in Kevin's voice suggested he had similar problems with the idea. 'Just a group I belong to. It's an important meeting.'

The thing with temps, Dominic had found, was you couldn't just threaten them with the sack. They always had something new to move onto, and no incentive to stay.

And, it was worth remembering, Kevin had screwed up almost every simple job Dominic had asked him to do in the last week. Sometimes, if you wanted a job done properly...

'Fine. Go. I'll fix it.'

The scrambling on the other end of the line suggested Kevin was already halfway out of the door. 'Yes, sir. Thank you.' He hung up.

Dominic gave the beer another wistful look. And then he called Shelley.

The wailing child in the background wasn't a good sign. 'Dominic, I am on maternity leave. I do not work for you right now.'

'I know that. But—'

'Are you sure? Because this is the fifth time you've called me this week.'

'In my defence, you weren't supposed to go on maternity leave for another two weeks.'

'I am very sorry that my son arrived early and disrupted your busy schedule.' She didn't sound very sorry, Dominic thought. She sounded sarcastic. 'Now, what do you want? And quickly.'

'The Americans. Kat cancelled all our bookings and—'

'Told you not to sleep with her.'

'And I need to find them somewhere to stay and someone to look after them while they're in London.'

'Yes,' Shelley said. 'You do.'

'Can you help?' He hated begging. Hated admitting he needed the assistance. But Shelley had been with him for five years. She knew how he worked, what he needed. She was part of the company.

Or she had been, until she left him.

She obviously still had more loyalty than Kevin, though. Sighing, she said, 'I'll check my contacts and text you some hotel names and tour companies you can try. But you'll have to wait until I've got Micah back off to sleep.'

'Thank you.'

'And this is the last time, Dominic. You're going to have to learn to work with Kevin.'

'I could just hire someone else,' Dominic mused. The thought of a whole year with Kevin was untenable.

'Fine. Whatever. I don't care. Just stop calling me!' Shelley hung up.

Placing his phone on the bar, Dominic looked at the bottle of beer. How long did it take to get a child off to sleep, anyway? He might as well have a drink while he was waiting. But, as he reached for the bottle, a woman boosted herself up onto the stool next to him and smiled.

Raising the bottle to his lips, Dominic took in the low-cut blouse, too-tight skirt and wild dark hair framing large hazel eyes. The smile on her wide lips was knowing, and he wondered if she'd recognised him. What she wanted from him. A drink. A night. A story to sell. She wouldn't be the first, whatever it was.

And whatever it was, she wouldn't get it. He'd made a mistake, letting Kat close enough to damage his reputation. It wasn't one he intended to make again—certainly not for one night with a pretty girl with an agenda.

But, to his surprise, the first words she said were, 'Sounds like you have a problem, my friend. And I think I can help you out.'

It wasn't the way she normally got work, but there was a lot to be said for serendipity, Faith decided. Walking into an airport bar, jobless and broke, and hearing a guy talk about how he needed a London tour guide and hotel rooms? That was an opportunity that was meant to be.

'And how, exactly, do you intend to do that?' the guy asked. He didn't look quite as convinced by coincidence as she was.

Faith held out a hand. 'I'm Faith. I'm a tour guide. I know London even better than I know Italy and Rome, and I've been running tours here for a year and a half. And it just so happens that I've finished one tour today, and I have a break before my next one.' She didn't mention the slight hiccup in her heartbeat at the idea of going home to London. Probably it would be fine. She could be in and out in a week or so, heading off on a plane to sunnier, less panic-inducing climes.

Besides, at this point, it wasn't as if she had a lot of other options.

'Dominic,' the guy said, taking her hand. He looked familiar, she realised. But then, after a while, all men in grey suits looked the same, didn't they? Maybe not quite as attractive as this one, though. His gaze was cool and evaluating. The high-end suit said 'successful businessman', the loosened tie said 'workaholic' and the beer said 'long day'. She could work with all of those. 'And how, exactly, do you know I need a tour guide?'

'I eavesdropped.' Faith shrugged, then realised the move strained her struggling blouse a little more than was wise in a professional environment. Maybe she should have left the necktie on.

'Not exactly the key quality I look for in an employee.' He frowned down at her cleavage with more distaste than she was used to seeing in a man.

'Really?' Faith asked. 'Someone who listens even when they're not required to and anticipates your needs? I've always found that rather useful.'

It was funny, Faith thought, the way you could watch someone re-evaluate you, and see the change in their attitude as a result. When she'd first sat down, she'd known all he saw was boobs and hair. Then she'd offered to help him, and his expression had changed from dismissive to interested. And now...now he was really intrigued.

'Okay, so, we've established I need a tour guide. I also need seven luxury hotel rooms in a central London five-star hotel.'

Thank goodness for airport Wi-Fi.

Logging into her browser from her smartphone, Faith scrolled through to the late booking accommodation site Marco always used, and set her search parameters. 'For tomorrow?'

Dominic nodded. 'Staying six nights.'

There weren't a lot of options, so Faith just presented him with the best one. 'How about the Greyfriars?' She turned the screen for him to see the eye-watering price, next to the photo of a hotel suite larger than the flat she'd shared with Antonio in Rome.

A slight widening of the eyes, a tight smile, and Faith knew he was re-evaluating her again. Good. She could be useful to him, and he could be even more useful to her. Time he realised that.

'The Greyfriars should work.'

Faith tapped a few more buttons on her tiny screen. 'I've reserved the rooms. Do you want to trust me with your credit card information, or call and speak with them directly?'

He raised his eyebrows, even as he pulled his wallet from his jacket pocket. For a moment, Faith thought he might actually hand it over, but then he picked up his phone, too. 'Give me the number.'

Grabbing her well used red notebook from her bag, Faith scribbled down both the phone number of the hotel and the reservation reference, and pushed the page across to him.

While he spoke with the receptionist, Faith ordered herself a glass of wine, hoping that Dominic would be impressed enough by her efficiency that she wouldn't have to rely on her last twenty euros for much longer.

So. She'd got the man his hotel rooms; surely he had to offer her the tour guide job now, right? Which meant his next question would be 'What do you want?' She needed to formulate an answer—one that didn't let on exactly how much more she needed his help than he needed hers.

What did she want? For Antonio never to have found out who she really was. For Marco not to have done a bunk. For her parents to be normal middle-class people. Teachers, perhaps. People who fitted in, which her parents certainly did not. She wanted to not have to worry that every camera or phone she saw might be about to send her picture soaring around the realms of social media, ready to be identified as Lady Faith, the Missing Heiress.

She wanted to have never been caught on camera leaving that hotel room, three years ago. That was a big one.

But right now, she'd settle for a ride back to London, a hotel room for the week, meals and drinks included, and maybe a small salary at the end of the job. Enough to tide her over until she found her next gig. It wouldn't take long; she was good at her job, she enjoyed it, and people liked her. That was important in the events and tourism industry.

'Thank you for your assistance,' Dominic said, and put down his phone. Faith looked up with a bright smile. Okay, she didn't really know who this guy was, or what business he was in, but he could afford seven rooms at the Greyfriars, so he could get her out of Rome without having to call her family, which was the most important thing.

'Let me tell you a little bit more about what I need,' he said, and Faith nodded, her best attentive face on. 'My name is Lord Dominic Beresford, and I run a number of businesses from my family's estates.' Faith's stomach clenched at the name. Of course he looked familiar. She'd probably seen him on the society pages a dozen times when she lived in London, usually next to photos of her mother looking tipsy behind her fake smile, or her father charming another man's wife. Or even of Faith herself, leaving the current London hotspot on the arm of someone very unsuitable. Lord Beresford, on the other hand, was always immaculately dressed and frowning.

'I have six American businessmen and -women arriving in London tomorrow morning,' Dominic went on, oblivious to the way her stomach was rolling. 'I need you to meet and greet them, plan entertainment for the hours they're not going to be in meetings, and accompany them on tours, the theatre, whatever you come up with.' He gave her a sharp look. 'Can you do it?'

Spend a week in the company of a man who could at any moment realise exactly who she was and expose her, all while avoiding anyone she knew in London, and working at the same time?

'Of course I can.'

Dominic nodded. 'Then we'll talk salary on the plane. Finish your drink; we'll go get you a ticket. But first...' He picked up his phone again, tapped a speed-dial number, and waited.

Was that crying Faith could hear in the background?

'Shelley?' Dominic said, almost shouting to be heard. 'Don't worry. I've fixed it.'

CHAPTER TWO

HE'D ASKED THE wrong question, Dominic realised, later that evening. He shouldn't have asked Faith if she could do the job. He should have asked her if she knew how to be quiet.

The answer was now startlingly obvious: no.

She'd chattered through the ticket line. All through security. Yammered on in the first-class lounge. And kept talking all the way to the gate and onto the plane.

And now they were cruising at thirty-two thousand feet, the cabin lights were dimmed, and she was still asking questions.

'Have you taken clients on the London Eye before? What about up the Shard? I haven't done that yet, but I've read reports...'

Grabbing another file from his briefcase, in the vain hope that the growing stack of them on the table in front of him might suddenly make her realise he was trying to work here, Dominic tried to tune out the chatter from the seat beside him. It wasn't as if she took a breath long enough for him to answer anyway.

Why did she have to sit next to him? First class was practically empty. There were plenty of places for her to stretch out, watch a movie, sleep. Not talk.

'Do you know if they're theatre buffs? I can do some

research on what's the hottest show in town when we land. Or maybe the opera?'

Of course, there were plenty of other questions he should have asked, too. Like why she was so eager to come work for a total stranger for over a week. Did she need to get out of Rome? Or was she just homesick? Jobless? He should have asked for credentials, for references, for anything that proved who she was. He hadn't even managed a glimpse of her passport as she handed it over to the ticket clerk.

It wasn't like him to be so impulsive. Yes, he'd been in a corner and needed a quick fix. And okay, he'd wanted to prove to Shelley and Kevin that he could manage quite well without them, thank you. He was still the boss, after all.

But if he was honest with himself, he knew the real reason he'd hired Faith was because of her attitude. It took guts to walk up to a stranger in an airport and tell them to give you a job. Guts and desperation, probably. But if she had a reason for needing this job, she hadn't let on. She'd focused entirely on what she could do for him, and it had worked.

Coupled with her curvaceous, striking appearance, that courage and determination meant she'd probably go far, in whatever she decided to do—if her blunt, frank manner didn't get her into trouble first. She was the exact opposite of anything he'd look for in a woman normally, but Faith wasn't a woman. Not to him, anyway. She was an employee, and that was a completely different thing.

Of course, she wasn't exactly like his other employees, either. Shelley, outspoken as she could be now, hadn't started that way. For the first year she hadn't questioned anything, hadn't complained, hadn't offered an opinion. And she'd still never be seen dead in a skirt as tight as Faith's. No, Shelley was beige suits and pastel blouses, where Faith was red lipstick and high heels.

Dominic didn't even waste time on a mental comparison between Faith and Kevin.

'And, uh, actually…I should have asked…'

Good grief, was there a question she hadn't blurted out already?

With a sigh, Dominic looked up at her, only to find her plump lower lip caught between white teeth, and an uncertainty in her eyes for the first time since they met.

'Yes?' he asked, surprised by her sudden change in demeanour.

'Will you want me to stay at the hotel with your guests?'

He blinked. 'Well, yes. That would be easiest.' He'd need to get an extra room, he realised. Efficient as she seemed to be, he could hardly leave his most important clients with a stranger for the next week. No, he'd need to stay there too, that much was obvious. But if Faith was staying in the hotel, at least he could delegate their more mundane requirements to her. 'Unless you have a pressing need to stay somewhere else?'

'No, no, it's not that.' She gave him a smile, an understated, nothing to worry about here smile. One he didn't entirely trust. His mother had smiled like that, in the weeks before she left. 'It's just that I've been living in Rome for the last year and a half. I don't actually *have* anywhere to stay in London.'

It was only when the muscles in his shoulders relaxed that Dominic realised they'd tensed at all. Of course she didn't have anywhere to stay. That made perfect sense.

It didn't entirely explain why she'd been so eager to leave Rome on a moment's notice, with only a pull-along suitcase for company, but Dominic was sure he could persuade her to tell him that story, in time. He was a very persuasive man when he put his mind to it. And he *really* wanted to know what Faith was running away from. Just in case it was something he needed to defend his reputation against.

'You'll have a room at the hotel,' he promised, before realising something else. 'But we'll need to see if we can get one for tonight, too.'

Faith glanced down at her watch, and he knew what she was thinking. By the time they got into London it would be the early hours. Anyone checking in last minute to a hotel at that kind of time wasn't usually there on business. Not the legitimate sort, anyway.

'Maybe it would be best if I checked into one of the airport hotels?' she suggested. 'That way, I'll be on hand ready to meet your clients there in the morning.'

It made perfect sense. And suddenly Dominic couldn't face the drive into London, all the way to his penthouse apartment, just in time to wake up and pack ready to move into a hotel for the week. 'Good plan,' he said. 'As soon as we land you can book us both in.'

She flashed him a smile, this one more confident, more teasing. 'Does that mean you're trusting me with your credit card at last?'

He'd have to, he realised. She'd need a method of payment for all the things he'd asked her to do, to set up. Even if it was just having some petty cash to make sure she could buy the Americans a coffee if they needed it.

'I'll call the bank in the morning, get you set up with a card linked to my expenses account.' The bank knew him well, and he certainly gave them enough business to request a favour. They could monitor the activity on that card. 'In the meantime, I'll provide you with some petty cash. A thousand should do it.'

'Right.' Her eyes were wide, he realised. She hadn't expected him to actually hand over his money. She had to realise, from the way he'd casually paid for her incredibly expensive last-minute seat in first class, that money wasn't much of an object to him these days. But it obviously was to her.

As was trust. Interesting.

Dominic had a feeling he had a lot still to learn about his latest employee.

But that could wait until London. 'And now, if you don't mind, I've got some work I'd like to finish before we land.'

She nodded, silent, and he turned back to his file, enjoying the peace and quiet. Who knew that all he had to do to stop Faith talking was offer her money and trust? If he'd have guessed, he would have tried it hours ago.

She couldn't just sit there. Apart from anything else, it was boring. What was in those files that Dominic found so fascinating?

Faith wasn't a sitting still and waiting kind of girl. She got fidgety.

Besides, the longer she sat there, staring out of the aeroplane window at the night skies, the more she imagined, in detail, every possible way this whole plan could go wrong. It wasn't a pretty list.

He wanted to get her a credit card. Which meant he'd need her full name. She'd managed to avoid him seeing her passport information, just, but he'd have to have it for the bank. What did she do? If she gave him a fake name, the bank might not authorise the card and she'd have to explain everything anyway. No, the only option was to give him her real name, minus the assorted titles, and hope he didn't recognise it.

At least Dominic didn't seem like the sort to spend his mornings reading the society pages, however often he appeared in them.

She needed to know more about him, Faith decided. If she knew who he was, what mattered to him, she might be able to predict his response if he figured out who she was. Would he drag her back to her parents by her hair, as her great-uncle had threatened? Or would he out her to the media, like Antonio had said he would? Or would he let her slip back out of the country, quiet and safe, to carry on living her own life?

If only she could be sure.

Faith sighed and, beside her, Dominic made a small irritated sound. One thing was clear: she wasn't going to find out all about her new employer by asking him questions when he was trying to work. No, she'd have to do this the modern way—Internet stalking. Surely the airport hotel would have free Wi-Fi?

'Do you have to think so loudly?' Dominic asked, reordering his papers again so half of them crept over the edge of the table, almost onto her lap.

'I'm pretty sure thinking is, by definition, a fairly quiet activity,' Faith said, shoving the papers back up onto the table.

'Not the way you do it.'

Right. Well, if she couldn't talk *or* think, maybe it was time to go and find something more interesting to do. Somewhere Dominic wasn't.

'Okay, let me out.' She nudged her elbow against his side, and he looked up in surprise.

'Where are you going?' he asked.

'Somewhere I can think without disturbing your hypersensitive hearing.' Yes, he was difficult and crazy, but he was at least paying for her to get back home. Best not to totally annoy him this early in the game.

Shuffling his papers back into a neat stack, Dominic slid out of his seat, into the wide, wide aisle. God, she'd missed first class.

'Don't get into any trouble,' he said, looking disturbingly like Great-Uncle Nigel.

Faith gave him her most winning, most innocent smile. 'Me? I never get into trouble.'

And then, leaving him looking utterly unconvinced, she sashayed through towards business class to find some more interesting people to annoy with her questions and her thinking.

He was being ridiculous. How could it be harder to concentrate without Faith beside him, fidgeting, talking and *thinking*, than it was when she was there?

But somehow, it was.

Pushing his files across the table, since he clearly wasn't going to be able to concentrate on them tonight, Dominic leant back in his seat and considered. Where would she have gone? They were on a plane, for heaven's sake. It wasn't as if she could have run away. If they'd been sitting in any other area of the aircraft, he'd have suspected her of running off to first class to try and win over the affections of a wealthy businessman.

He glanced around the small section of seats on his side of the curtain. No sign of her. The only other occupants—an elderly gentleman in a suit and a woman with a pashmina wrapped around her, almost covering her face—were both asleep.

Maybe she'd gone back to business class to find a new friend there. Maybe the promise of a job with him wasn't enough. Maybe she just needed him for the flight home, and now she'd moved onto looking for her next opportunity...

Dominic forced himself to stop that line of thought. Just because certain women behaved that way, taking what they wanted then running, leaving destruction in their path, didn't mean that Faith would. He should give her the benefit of the doubt. Hadn't he just told her he trusted her enough to hand over a significant amount of money? Of course, money came easy to him, these days. Reputation was much harder won.

On the other hand, she was his employee. His responsibility.

The only responsible thing to do, really, was go find her.

To Dominic's surprise, there was no sign of Faith in business class. He got some funny looks as he peered across darkened seats, trying to spot a dark, curly head, but he ignored them. Maybe she'd found a steward or something to talk to? At least she hadn't been heading the right way to try and bother the pilot...

Pushing through the curtain, business class gave way to economy, where the occasional empty seats ended, replaced by cramped and crowded rows of people. Many were sleeping—it was the middle of the night, after all—but there were more screens and lights on than in either of the other sections. Dominic supposed it was harder to get some shut-eye when you were crammed in like cattle.

Faith must have disappeared into the bathroom, he decided. He just hoped that she was alone—the last thing his reputation needed was an article in the press about him and his employee being banned from an airline for joining the mile-high club. It wouldn't matter to a reporter that Dominic hadn't been the man with Faith at the time. Those sort of details never did, he'd found.

But then, as he turned back to try and get some more work done before landing, he spotted her and stopped, just to watch.

She was crouched down at the front of the economy section, just beside the seats with the space for a baby's bassinet against the wall; he must have walked right past her on his way through. Her dark head was bent over a bundle in her arms, and when she looked up at the parents of the child she was holding, her face glowed. Smiling, she whispered away in rapid Italian, all while tucking in blankets and stroking the baby's fine, downy hair.

This wasn't what he'd expected. In fact, this wasn't even recognisable as the woman he'd hired. Except… As he got closer, he caught a few English words scattered in her conversation. Big Ben. Madame Tussauds. The Tube.

A smile tugged at the corner of Dominic's mouth. She was offering them tourist advice. Planning their trip to London with them.

Without drawing attention to himself, Dominic slipped past, back through the curtain to where his files were waiting.

Perhaps he had hired the right woman, after all.

CHAPTER THREE

IT TOOK FAITH a moment to remember where she was when she woke up the next morning. Smooth white cotton sheets, rain battering the window, the glow of a reading lamp she obviously hadn't managed to turn off before she passed out the night before. Definitely not the flat she'd shared with Antonio and, given the rain, probably not even Rome.

No, Faith knew that rain. Knew that cold splatter and relentless fall.

She was in England. London.

Exactly where she shouldn't be, ever again.

Faith buried her head deeper into the pillow, as if she could block out the grey and the rain and the sheer London-ness of it all. She hadn't had a choice, she reminded herself. She'd made the best decision she could in a difficult situation.

But she couldn't help but wonder about all the people she'd left behind when she ditched the city she loved the first time. Were they still there? What would she do if she saw one of them on the street? Turn and walk the other way, or brazen it out?

She guessed she wouldn't know unless it happened.

Hopefully it wouldn't. In and out, that was the key. Do the job, take the money and run.

So, back to the job. And her employer.

Dominic had chosen the most expensive of the airport hotels once they'd landed in Heathrow, which hadn't really surprised her at that point. To be honest, she could have slept in a chair in the terminal, she was so tired. But the blissfully soft pillows and firm mattress of the hotel room were a definite improvement.

Reluctantly pushing herself up into a seated position, shoulders resting against the headboard, she tried to wake up enough to get a handle on the day ahead. Dominic had said the Americans were arriving around eleven, and it was only eight-thirty. So she had plenty of time to shower, dress…wait. What was she going to wear? She had her uniforms from the Roman Holiday Tour Company, she had her going-out-for-dinner dress and she had some jeans and plain T-shirts. She hadn't exactly packed for corporate events when she'd left Rome. She'd packed for an overnight in London and then another tour.

It would have to be the uniforms, she supposed, for now at least. Maybe she could ask Dominic about an advance on her wages, or even a clothing allowance. Given the disapproving look he'd given her outfit in the bar the night before, she suspected he might be amenable.

A knock on the door dragged her thoughts away from her wardrobe and onto her growling stomach. Was that room service? Had she remembered to leave the breakfast card out the night before? She really hoped so. She was useless without a decent meal in the morning.

Swinging her legs out of bed, she glanced down at her rather skimpy red nightgown—a present from Antonio, of course. He never did have any concept of subtle. Still, she supposed that room service had probably seen much worse.

Except, when she yanked open the door with a smile, it wasn't room service.

Dominic's eyes travelled down over her body at an offensively quick speed. Any other man, Faith knew, would have lingered over her curves, outlined in red silk. Any other man would have enjoyed the view of her bare legs.

Her new employer, however, merely catalogued her attire and raised an eyebrow at her. 'Do you always open your door dressed like a lingerie model?'

Faith felt the heat flush to her face. 'I thought you were room service with breakfast.'

'I'm afraid if you want breakfast you'll have to get dressed. Assuming you have something more suitable to wear...' His eyes flicked over her shoulder to where her skirt and blouse from the day before lay draped over a chair. Faith winced when she noticed the pale pink lace bra lying on top of them.

'Actually, that was something I wanted to talk to you about...'

Dominic glanced at his watch. 'No time. Get dressed and we'll talk over coffee, before we head over to arrivals.'

'I thought your clients didn't get in until eleven?' Faith asked, confused.

'They don't.' Dominic was already walking away down the corridor. 'But you need a briefing before they arrive.'

He turned a corner and was gone. Apparently busy executives didn't have time to finish conversations properly. Or tell people where to meet them when they were decently dressed.

An elderly couple appeared at the end of the corridor and Faith realised, a little belatedly, that she was standing in the open in her really inappropriate nightie. Stepping back inside her room, she shut the door firmly behind her and headed for the shower.

Time to prove to Lord Dominic Beresford that she was capable of doing any job he needed doing, whatever she was wearing.

Good God, did she sleep in that every night? Even when she was alone and exhausted and straight off a plane, Faith managed to slip into a sexy little number for bed. Dominic shook his head. What kind of a devil temptress had he hired?

Unless, of course, she'd put it on especially for him that morning. Unless she planned to seduce and ruin him, just like Katarina had tried to do. Just like his mother had done to his father.

It was all still a little too neat. Dominic didn't believe in coincidences, or serendipity, or any of the other things Faith had chattered about on the plane, her smile too wide, her lips too tempting. She'd been in exactly the right place at exactly the right time and, in his experience, that sort of thing didn't happen without some forward planning.

Still, he did need a tour guide, and she seemed to be an adequate one. All he had to do was stay out of her way while she worked, and she'd never get the chance to put any sort of plans into action. It would be fine.

As soon as he could erase that image of her in fiery red silk from his brain.

Figuring she'd take an insane amount of time to shower and dress, Dominic headed down to the restaurant and ordered coffee while he perused the papers. He wasn't much for breakfast, but he'd grab a piece of toast or some fruit when Faith joined him. They had too much to discuss to waste time on food.

However she'd come into his life, and whatever she hoped to get out of it, the only thing that mattered to Dominic was that she did the job he hired her to do: take care of his clients. He knew his strengths weren't always in the socialising side of things—he'd generally rather be in his office. That was why his arrangement with Katarina had worked so well. She'd taken care of the smiling, small talk and looking interested side of things. He took care of the business.

Bloody Katarina. She was right up there with Shelley on his list of women determined to thwart him right now. He just hoped that Faith wouldn't be added to it before she and the Americans left at the end of next week.

Sooner than he'd expected, Faith appeared at the entrance to the hotel restaurant. She waved a hand in his direction but, instead of heading for his table, she made for the breakfast buffet.

Holding in a sigh, Dominic watched as she bypassed the platters of fruit and the glass containers full of cereal. Instead, she loaded up her plate with eggs, bacon, sausage, beans, fried bread…and grabbed a side plate for a couple of mini pastries, too.

Apparently those curves were made entirely of breakfast.

'Hungry?' he asked, eyebrow raised, as she finally made it to the table.

Depositing her plates, Faith ripped off a bite of *pain au chocolat* as she dropped into her seat. 'Starving. Do you think they'll bring me some tea?'

His mother's lessons in etiquette and good manners towards women were deeply ingrained, and Dominic found himself motioning over a waiter to request a pot

of tea and more coffee for himself before he even realised he was doing it.

'You've eaten already?' Faith asked, after swallow-
ing an enormous forkful of eggs and toast.

'I don't usually eat breakfast,' he replied, folding
his paper neatly across the middle and placing it on
the empty table beside them. 'Especially when I've an
important day ahead.'

'That's just when you need it,' Faith said, sounding
eerily like a nanny he'd had when he was eight.

'I've made it this far. I think I'll survive. Now. To
business.' Casting his gaze over her outfit, he was relieved to find it less revealing than the day before, and
certainly less fantasy-inducing than the silk concoction
she'd had on first thing. The skirt, he realised, was the
same as yesterday, but paired with a plain white T-shirt.
Still, while the higher neckline hid the very tempting
cleavage the blouse had displayed, it emphasised her
curves even more.

I'm not thinking about this. I am not *thinking about
this.*

Of any man alive, surely he knew better than most
the perils of giving in to temptation and forgetting obligations. Faith was here to work, and that was all. He
had to remember that.

'Yes. Work,' Faith said, bringing his attention back to
the topic at hand. 'I wanted to run through a few things
with you, actually.' To his surprise, she whipped a small
notebook from her bag, uncapped a pen and sat poised
to write down his answers. 'First, can your office send
me an itinerary for the week so I know exactly what
you've got planned for your guests, and I can work
around it? Also, it means I can make myself available
if anyone has any questions between meetings.'

'I'll ask Kevin to fax one over,' he said, trying to remember if Kevin even knew how to work the fax machine.

'Great. Once I have that, I'll put together a tentative itinerary and email it to you for your approval.'

'You'll need a laptop,' Dominic realised, belatedly.

'No need.' Pulling a tablet computer from her bag, she waved it at him. 'I use this.'

He blinked at her. 'Well, great. Okay then.'

'Next, do you have any background details on the clients themselves? Their lives, their families, their businesses, anything that I can use to get to know them?'

'You do realise you're a tour guide, not a dating service, right? You don't need to find them their perfect match.'

Her face turned stony, and he regretted the joke. She was trying to do a good job, after all. He should be encouraging her, not ridiculing her.

'These people are a long way from home for almost two whole weeks. It's my job to make sure they enjoy themselves and feel comfortable here. Knowing a little about them makes that easier. I'll talk to them myself when they arrive, of course, but a little forward knowledge would mean I can get going sooner.'

'Of course,' Dominic said contritely. 'Well, their businesses I can tell you about. But, as for the rest of it...' He spread his hands out. 'Katarina used to handle that sort of thing, I'm afraid.'

Faith paused with her mini cinnamon swirl halfway to her mouth. Katarina. That was a new name. 'Is Katarina your secretary?' If so, she could call and ask her for all the gossip.

'No. Not my secretary.' Dominic shifted in his chair,

looking sorry he'd ever mentioned the woman. Not a secretary. Then...

'Your wife?'

He sighed, and reached for the coffee. 'My ex-fiancée, actually. But, more pertinently, she runs the company we usually use for this sort of thing.'

'But not this time,' Faith said.

'No. Not this time.'

'Because you split up.'

Dominic gave her an exasperated look. 'Can't you ever take a hint to stop asking questions?'

Faith shrugged unapologetically. 'I like to know exactly where I stand with things. Makes life a lot less complicated.'

'Well, she doesn't matter any more. She's gone. You're here now to take her place,' Dominic said, entirely matter-of-fact.

Faith felt a peculiar squirming feeling in her stomach. 'As a tour guide. Not as your fiancée.'

Dominic looked up, appalled. 'That goes without saying!'

Faith flushed. 'You don't have to be quite so horrified at the prospect,' she muttered.

'Right. No. I just meant...' He sighed. 'This is a business arrangement, for both of us. Katarina...she's out of the picture now, and I'm afraid you can't really call her for insights on our guests.'

Now, that was interesting. Surely the woman would have an assistant or something that Faith could call for some notes. For Dominic to be so certain she wouldn't help, something pretty dramatic had to have happened between them.

'Bad break up?' she asked.

'The worst,' Dominic groaned, and for the first

time since she'd met him in that airport bar he seemed human. Normal. As if he had actual emotions and feelings, rather than a sensor that told him when to be disapproving of something.

'Want to talk about it?' she asked.

'Not even a little bit.' He didn't leave any room for discussion.

Oh well. Human moment over.

'Okay, well, if you can't tell me about them as people, you must be able to tell me why they're here. What's the very important business you have with them?'

Dominic leaned back in his chair. 'I'm looking to expand the activities and operations we have running on the Beresford estate. We're considering buying up some neighbouring land to build on, as well as utilising the Beresford family's London properties.'

In which case, Faith thought, they'd be one of the only aristocratic families to actually *increase* their family estates in generations. 'So these guys are your investors?'

Dominic nodded. 'Potential investors. But also potential clients. They want to see what we have on offer, and possibly use Beresford Hall in the future for international corporate retreats.'

'Okay, that helps. Now, they've visited London before, right? I don't suppose you've got a record of what they've seen and done...?' Dominic winced. 'No. Of course not.'

Faith sighed. Looked as if she was doing this the hard way. In which case, she really needed a kick-ass outfit to give her confidence.

'Okay, since you can't actually give me any practical help to do my job—'

'I gave you the job itself, didn't I?' Dominic's words

came out almost as a growl, and Faith decided to change tack.

'And in order that I can do it to the best of my ability and present the right impression of your company to your clients…I was wondering if there might be some sort of clothing allowance involved…'

His eyes did that quick flash over her body again, and Faith gave thanks she hadn't put the other, scoop neck, T-shirt on that morning. Not that he'd have noticed, of course. All he seemed to care about was that she wasn't wearing some boring suit.

'You're right,' Dominic said. 'I do need you to make the right impression.'

Faith perked up a bit. 'So you'll give me money to go shopping?'

Dominic shook his head, and the smile that spread across his face was positively devilish. 'No. I'll take you shopping to find something suitable.'

Something suitable. Faith slumped down into her chair a little.

Why did she suspect that Dominic's idea of 'suitable' would translate into something she'd never usually wear in a million years?

CHAPTER FOUR

'I'M NOT WEARING THAT.'

Dominic sighed and turned towards his newest employee with his best 'I'm the boss' face in place. Faith stared back at him, unaffected.

He hadn't expected the airport to be a shopping Mecca—he was normally more concerned with finding a quiet spot in the first-class lounge to work when he passed through. Still, he knew that there were plenty of shops, and that people enjoyed taking advantage of them.

Sadly, it hadn't occurred to him that most of them would be selling holiday apparel, especially at this time of year. Options for professional attire were somewhat limited.

'It's a suit, Faith. An inoffensive grey suit. It's perfectly respectable. What's wrong with it?'

'What's wrong with it?' Eyebrows raised, she parroted his words back at him. 'It's a suit. A perfectly respectable, inoffensive suit. Do I look like the sort of woman who likes to appear respectable and inoffensive?'

'Well, you don't look like a Beresford employee yet, if that's what you mean.' Hooking the clothes hanger back onto the rail, he smiled apologetically at the shop assistant and followed Faith back out of the shop, into

the crowded terminal. A large clock, hanging somewhere overhead like a countdown, told him his clients
would be arriving in less than an hour, and Faith still
looked like a waitress in a university bar.

'Look, here's the deal,' he said, waiting until she
stopped walking and turned to face him before con-
tinuing. 'If you want to work for me, you have to look
like a professional, grown-up woman.'

'As opposed to?' Faith asked, eyebrows raised.

How to put it... In the end, Dominic decided to err
on the side of caution. 'This is a bigger, more important
job. You can't just look like a tour guide.'

Faith's mouth tightened, and Dominic prepared himself for an onslaught of objections. But instead, eyes
narrowed, she held out a hand. 'Give me the money.'

'What?'

She rubbed her fingers together. 'Hand over the cash
you would have spent on that hideous suit. Then go and
get yourself a coffee.'

'And what are you going to do?' Against his better
judgement, Dominic was already pulling the notes from
his wallet. It hadn't been a cheap suit.

'I'm going to show you that you don't have to spend
a fortune on something that looks the same as what everyone else is wearing to look professional.' She took
the money and tucked it into her bag. 'I'll meet you over
there in forty-five minutes.' Then, waving her hand in the
direction of a coffee shop, she walked off, leaving him
a few hundred pounds lighter, and minus one employee.

Apparently, she'd taken the trust he'd promised her,
and run with it.

If there was one thing Faith knew, it was how to shop
for clothes. Growing up, her mother had instilled in

her the need to look polished, appropriate and, above all, expensive. In the years when her father had spent most of the estate income on a horse that didn't come in or a woman who visited far too frequently, wearing something new and fabulous to every occasion could be something of a problem. And once her parents had finally admitted that the money was gone, and Faith said goodbye to her boarding school blazer, trying to fit in at the local secondary school, even in the same polyester skirt as everyone else, had been a whole new challenge.

There, clothes had been the least of her worries. There, she'd been the rich kid with no money, the posh kid who swore like a sailor, the girl who thought she was too good for them, even if she didn't. There'd been no place for her at all, no little corner to fit in, and the loneliness of it still burned if she thought about it too much. She'd spent lessons daydreaming about being someone else. About leaving home, her parents and her title behind her. Of being Just Faith, instead of Lady Faith.

She'd thought she'd managed it, once she left school and moved to London. Thought she was her own person for once. Except it was so easy to fall in with people who she realised, too late, only wanted her for her title. Women who had closets of spare outfits to dress her up in, dresses and skirts that cost a fortune but barely had the structural integrity to survive a night of dancing and drinking at whatever club they used her name to get into.

They definitely weren't the sort of clothes Dominic wanted her wearing on this job.

Later, living abroad, alone and with only her seasonal tour earnings to keep her, clothing hadn't been a priority. She'd been her own person for the first time ever, and she hadn't had to dress a certain way to prove it.

The sense of freedom, of relief, was enough. So she had uniforms for work and a small, flexible, casual wardrobe for the rest of the time.

Dominic had been right about one thing—not that she'd admit it to him—this new job required new clothes.

But she'd be damned if she was spending the next week and a half in one plain, boring suit.

She didn't have long, so she worked a strike attack formula, identifying the three closest mid-range high street stores most likely to stock the sort of thing she needed. In the first, she picked up two skirts—one grey, one black—and a couple of bright cardigans. In the next, a jacket, three blouses and a lightweight scarf. The last shop took the largest chunk of her money, but in return provided her with a pair of low heels that looked professional, but that she could walk miles in. When she mixed in the plain T-shirts, underwear, bag, dress, make-up and jewellery she'd brought with her from Rome, she thought she was pretty much prepared for anything Lord Dominic Beresford could throw at her that week.

Stepping out of the last shop, laden with bags, she checked her watch. Five minutes left. Just enough time to change.

It was strangely gratifying to walk into the coffee shop and realise that Dominic hadn't even recognised her. He glanced up when she walked in, but his gaze flicked quickly away from her and back to the clock on the wall. He expected her to be late.

Dumping her bags on an empty chair, she dropped into the seat opposite him and grinned as his eyes widened. This time, he studied her carefully, taking in the jacket and blouse—worn over her white T-shirt to en-

sure maximum modesty in the cleavage department—
and the way she'd pinned her hair back from her face.

She gave him a minute to appreciate the transformation, then said, 'This works for you?'

Dominic nodded.

'Great.' Grabbing his coffee from in front of him,
she drained the last inch of caffeine. 'Then let's go meet
your clients.'

He had to stop looking at her. What kind of a professional impression did it make if he couldn't stop staring
at his employee? It was just…a transformation. Faith
looked respectable, efficient, and yet still utterly herself. And he still didn't quite understand how she'd managed to make his money stretch to the bags and bags of
shopping he'd had to send back to the hotel before they
headed to arrivals.

Now, while his driver loaded up their suitcases and
Faith's shopping at the hotel, they were waiting in the
arrivals hall for the next flight in from JFK. He could
have sent a driver to meet them, Dominic supposed, but
Kat had always hammered home the importance of the
personal touch. And since she wasn't here to be personal
any longer, that just left him. And Faith.

His gaze slid left again, taking in the way she gripped
her fingers tightly in her other hand. Was she nervous?
Did Faith really get nervous? It seemed unlikely.

'They're a nice bunch,' he said awkwardly, in an attempt to set her mind at ease.

'I'm sure.'

'They'll like you.'

She rolled her eyes at him. 'Of course they will.
Being likeable is part of my job description.'

'Really?' Dominic glanced at her again. 'You don't seem to be trying that hard with me.'

Faith flapped a hand at him. 'Don't lie, you adore me. Besides, you matter less.'

'I am the boss,' he reminded her. Just in case she'd forgotten. He was starting to wonder…

'Yeah. So you'll be taking care of them in meetings and things, right? I'll be with them the rest of the time. When they're having fun. So it's important they think I'm a fun person to be around. You'll probably be back in the office by then anyway, so what do you care?'

It should set his mind at ease, Dominic thought, knowing that she wasn't expecting him to be around all the time, holding her hand through this job. She obviously believed she was capable enough to get on with it alone. And, against the odds, he was starting to believe that too.

So why was he mentally reshuffling his calendar to figure out which evenings he could join them on their tours and outings?

'You're right,' he said, shaking away the uncomfortable thought. 'As long as you keep them entertained and happy, that's all that matters.'

'Good.' Faith nodded, then sucked in a breath as the words and numbers on the display board changed again. 'Because they're here.'

She was not afraid. She *was* not afraid. She was *not* afraid.

She'd done this a million times before. The meet and greet was the most important part, sure—people tended to stick with their first impressions, even when they claimed not to. But she was good at this. Good at smiling and welcoming and helping and making people feel at home.

So why were her hands clammy?

Maybe it was the clothes. Maybe she should have gone with the stupid suit…

'That's them,' Dominic said, and then it was too late to worry about any of it anyway, because they were surging forward into handshakes and smiles and polite greetings. Faith beckoned over the driver who'd met them in the arrivals hall to start collecting bags onto a trolley, glad of something real and useful to do. Something she knew and understood. How could she have thought that looking after a group of high-powered businesspeople in London would be the same as shepherding holidaying Brits around Italy? They were already launching into conversations with Dominic that she couldn't even begin to follow. The three letter acronyms alone were baffling.

The drive into London, in a spacious limo complete with high-end coffee machine, at least gave her a chance to get her latest charges straight in her head. There was Henry, large and jocular—easy to remember, as long as she kept picturing Henry VIII when she looked at him. Next was Bud, skinnier in the face but a little rotund around the middle. Like a bottle of beer. Perfect.

The first two names fixed, she turned to the next pair. Both in navy suits, both dark-haired, both serious-looking. Thank God one of them wore glasses or she'd be getting them confused all week. Their names, however, were even easier—an improbable ice cream concoction of Ben and Jerry. As long as she remembered that Jerry had the glasses, she was golden.

The last two of Dominic's clients were easy, too. The blonde woman in the fantastic red suit was Marie, which made Faith think of Marilyn, which made her think of Monroe. And the brunette in the more severe black trouser suit with spectacular heels was Terri, who could just be the one she couldn't think of a great mnemonic for. Five out of six wasn't bad.

With everyone straight in her head, Faith settled back in her seat to nurse her espresso, and try to make some sort of sense of the conversation. She followed the discussion about land purchase and architects all right, until they started throwing out figures and referencing forms. She sighed to herself and decided she needed to have attended at least six months of previous meetings to even begin to understand.

'I'm guessing this is kinda dull for you,' Ben—no, glasses! Jerry—said, leaning in to whisper close to her ear.

'Not dull,' Faith objected. 'Just…not my area of expertise.'

Jerry's eyes flashed down to her blouse. 'And what exactly is that? Dominic didn't say.'

'Faith is your tour guide for the week,' Dominic said sharply, from the other end of the car. Faith looked up in surprise; she hadn't realised he was paying any attention to her. And how had he even heard Jerry from there?

Suddenly all attention was on her. Plastering on her best social smile, Faith said, 'That's right. So if you've any thoughts on places you'd like to go, things you'd like to see, just let me know!'

'Oh, I can think of a couple,' Jerry murmured, still looking at her breasts. Faith shuffled a little further away, until her leg pressed up against the car door.

Looking up, she saw Dominic glaring at her. He couldn't have heard Jerry's latest comment, but surely he had to know this wasn't her idea?

Or not. Turning his attention back to his clients, Dominic launched into another highly dense and baffling business conversation. Faith listened for a moment until she spotted Marie giving her a sympathetic smile. Then, tuning out the figures and the jargon, she pulled her tablet from her bag and started planning the week ahead.

She might not understand Dominic's job, but she was damn good at her own, thank you.

Dominic needed to get out of cars and hotels and into the office. How was he expected to concentrate on the finer details of the outstanding contract when one of his clients was hitting on Faith?

She'd handled it well, professionally even, but he was under no illusions that she wouldn't let rip if the guy pushed his luck. And quite rightly, too. Perhaps he should have a little word with Jerry...

The Greyfriars Hotel was a hit with his guests, proving Faith's knowledge of the luxury hotel market spot on. Procuring an extra room for himself wasn't difficult—although booking the penthouse suite seemed a little excessive even to him, given he had his own apartment just across town. Still, it looked as if it would be a long week. He'd probably need a luxurious space to relax at night.

'So,' Faith said as she handed out keycards, 'I know you've got meetings planned this afternoon, but what would you like to do this evening? Sleep off your jet lag, or go out and party?'

Dominic was secretly hoping for the sleeping option, but the Americans all seemed to be up for a party.

Faith clapped her hands together. 'Great! I'll make sure to come up with something really special.'

Maybe he didn't have to go. After all the meetings in Rome, plus this afternoon to get through, he could really use the time in the office. Surely Faith would be okay without him?

But then he saw Jerry sidling up to Faith with his spare keycard in hand.

Stepping closer, he heard her say, 'Oh, I wouldn't worry. If you lose it, the hotel can make you another one.' She pushed the card back into Jerry's hand, and Dominic gave a mental cheer.

As Jerry stalked off towards his room, not looking particularly beaten, Dominic leant in towards Faith. 'Count me in for whatever tonight's activity is.'

She turned to him and scowled. 'Don't think I can handle it by myself?'

He grinned. 'Oh, I'm certain that you can. I just want to watch the show.'

The smile she gave him in return was positively devilish, and he didn't even try not to watch as she walked towards the lifts, hips swinging.

Maybe he wouldn't have that word with Jerry. It might be far more satisfying to watch Faith cut him down herself.

He'd just make sure he was on hand in case she needed any assistance.

CHAPTER FIVE

HER HOTEL ROOM was bigger than most of the apartments she'd lived in since leaving home, but somehow Faith still found herself down in the hotel coffee bar, just off the lobby, as she planned out the week's entertainment. She told herself it was because the Wi-Fi connection was faster, or because she'd be able to see the clients and Dominic arriving back at the hotel after their meetings. But actually, it was just a whole lot less lonely than sitting upstairs on her own.

She missed Antonio. Well, actually, that wasn't true. She didn't miss *him* exactly. More the idea of him. What she'd thought he was. A future, a family, a proper place in the world. A life that revolved around who she really was, who she wanted to be—not what other people expected of her.

Well, now she'd just have to find her own new place to belong. Wasn't as if she hadn't done it before. Maybe, if she did a good enough job, Dominic would take her on full-time, replacing the infamous Katarina on a more long-term basis.

Except that would put her closer to her old life than she was comfortable with. No, better to get the job done then move on. Again.

Faith's finger hovered over the touch screen of her

tablet, ready to type in her search for availability at London tourist hot spots that evening. But instead she found herself typing in the name Dominic Beresford.

She shouldn't feel guilty about this, she told herself, as page after page of results scrolled up. She was researching a new employer—standard procedure. Dominic would probably have done the same to her, although hopefully using the name Faith Fowler, one she'd made her own on the Continent. The only stories of interest about her were tall tales of the Italian landscape, and reviews of popular tourist destinations. Nothing to alarm him, and absolutely no photos.

There were lots of photos of Dominic, though. Photos of him glowering at the camera, as flashbulbs went off around him. Photos of him with an icy-cool blonde on his arm, almost as tall as he was, perfect pout in place for the paparazzi. That must be Katarina, she supposed.

Lady Katarina Forrester, in fact, according to the caption. Faith didn't know her, she didn't think, but that wasn't hugely surprising. She'd never been particularly enthusiastic about socialising with the aristocratic set—at least, not the respectable ones—whatever her mother's dreams of her finding a perfect, financially supportive match amongst them. There hadn't been a space for her there. Her place at boarding school hadn't been the only thing she lost when the money was gone.

Her finger paused over another link. This one was harder to justify. This one, if she was honest, was just Faith being incurably nosy. As usual. It really wasn't any of her business what Katarina Forrester got up to, or why she'd split up with Dominic.

Of course, she pressed it anyway.

And was instantly glad that she'd turned off the sound on the tablet. The video that sprang to life was really not one to be watching in public. Eyes wide, she paused it, then stared for a moment longer before closing the window down. That had to be Katarina, with that long blonde hair let loose from the chignon it had been contained by in every other photo. But the naked guy there with her? Definitely not Dominic.

Well, she supposed that answered the question of why they'd broken up. And it kind of made her wonder exactly what she'd find if she Googled her own name. Possibly best not to know.

Except…she was back in Britain, working the kind of job that might get her spotted at any minute. Wasn't it better to know what was out there waiting for her if she was recognised?

Before she could change her mind, Faith tapped out her real name in the search bar and waited to see what popped up, apprehension stirring in her chest.

At the top of the page, a row of photos loaded. Two of her looking bleary-eyed in a too-short dress, blinking at the camera as she left some nightclub. The rest…all from that night. Or, rather, the morning after.

God, was it really even her? She barely recognised the woman she was now in the girl on the screen. She'd thrown away the clothes she wore in the photos—the tight black jeans and the corset top, moulding her curves and pushing up her breasts. Her hair was shorter than it was now, just curling around her jawbone. The hotel name, high end and far more expensive than she'd have been able to afford on her own, was clearly visible in the back of the shots.

And on her arm, Jared Hawkes, a little too pale and scowling, but otherwise giving no indication of the hellish night before. Or that he was about to go home and beg his wife for another chance.

No, the photo looked exactly like what everyone had believed it was—a money-grabbing girl stealing a famous, and famously troubled, rock star away from his patient, wonderful wife and adoring kids.

The guilt had faded over the years. She'd made a lot of mistakes when she was younger, sure, but who hadn't? And this one, that one time, she really hadn't done anything wrong, as much as the world's media had tried to convince her—and everyone else—otherwise. It had taken her a while to accept that and forgive herself, after she dropped out of the public eye. But she was done with guilt. All she had left now was the resentment, and the pain of the injustice.

Faith clicked the browser closed. She didn't need to see any more.

She took a large gulp of coffee and tried to clear her head. Time to get back to the matter at hand—finding somewhere to take the Americans that evening.

She took her time perusing the usual websites, and also reading the best London blogs, to get some more unusual ideas. She'd forgotten how much there was to do and see in London, how much she loved being there. Sure, Rome was romantic as hell and had plenty to offer, but London…it was more of a patchwork. More bits and pieces and scraps from all across history, and across humanity. She liked that in a city.

By the time the hotel lobby doors opened to reveal chattering Americans, she'd worked up a decent plan for the week and got some provisional bookings in place. The name 'Lord Beresford' had opened plenty of doors she suspected might have stayed closed to Faith Fowler, Event Planner and Tour Guide, and while she'd vowed not to use her own title for the purpose of getting ahead, she had no qualms about using Dominic's.

Pushing aside her empty coffee cup—the third of the afternoon—she packed up her notes and tablet and headed out to greet the Americans before they disappeared up to their rooms to change.

'How did the meetings go?' she asked Dominic as his clients got in the lift on the other side of the lobby.

He shrugged. 'As well as I could hope, I suppose.'

Which sounded rather Eeyore-ish to her. Maybe he was depressed. After all, he'd just lost his fiancée to a muscly premiership footballer in a YouTube video. Hardly surprising if he felt a bit down about things. 'Well, I'm sure they'll all be on board with anything you propose after the evening I've got in store for them.'

He raised his eyebrows at her, and his forehead crinkled up. 'Really? Do I get to know the plan in advance?'

'You kinda have to,' Faith replied. 'I need you to pay for it. They're holding the reservation for another hour.'

Dominic fished in his jacket pocket and pulled out his wallet. Opening it, he pulled out a shiny silver card with the name 'Beresford Estate Expense Account' emblazoned on it, and handed it to her.

Faith stared at the card, even as she noticed the slip of paper with it. 'Memorise the PIN and destroy that paper,' he said. Then, when she just kept looking at it, he added, 'Go on. Don't you have a reservation to confirm?'

Faith swallowed. 'Don't you want to know what I've got planned for the evening?'

Dominic's smile was wicked. 'I trust you. Surprise me.'

Later that evening, as Dominic stared at the limited wardrobe he'd brought to the hotel, he regretted not asking Faith to share the plan for the evening. At least then he'd know if he needed the dinner jacket or if an ordinary suit would suffice. Or if whatever she had arranged would be more comfortable in jeans… Surely she'd have mentioned if they needed any sort of special outfits, though. Right?

Why hadn't he let her tell him?

Sighing, Dominic dropped to sit on the edge of the bed, tie in hand. The reason, if he was honest with himself, was simply that she'd looked so excited about her plans. Standing there in her bright red blouse, with her hair tied back, she'd bobbed excitedly up and down on her toes. And just the idea that she was trying so hard to get this right, to do a good job…he wanted her to have a moment of glory when she pulled it off.

If she pulled it off.

He should have checked. He should be approving all the plans for the week. He would with any other new supplier or contractor. So why was it different with Faith?

Because Faith was different, he answered himself. Faith was so many worlds away from Kat and the way she worked. Faith, for whatever reason, needed this job, and needed to do it well. And he was going to trust her and let her get on with it.

Even if she could be using his credit card for anything right now. She could be on her way to the airport and back to Italy. Or anywhere.

No. Faith wanted this job; that much he was sure of. Still, they'd only talked vaguely about budgets on the plane, and Faith didn't seem the sort to be constrained by vague limits when the perfect opportunity for fun showed up. Although she'd been pretty canny with his money when she went clothes shopping.

He should have more faith.

Groaning at the unintentional mental pun, Dominic lay back on the bed and wished it was eight o'clock and time to meet in the lobby already.

In the end, he was twenty minutes early, dressed in a suit and clean shirt, no tie—although he had one in his pocket in case of emergency. Compromise, he'd decided, was the name of the game. Something the Americans could stand to learn at the negotiating table, actually.

He was early, but Faith was earlier, already standing in the lobby, dressed in a black dress that skimmed her knees, and with a red cardigan over it that hid the neckline. Respectable, but not too formal. Maybe he could ditch the tie at reception...

'You're early,' she said, smiling at him as he approached. 'Too impatient to wait any longer?'

'Something like that,' Dominic admitted. Up close, he could see the red lipstick that made her mouth even wider and more tempting than normal. And he was studiously ignoring the way her black heels made her legs look endless.

Rifling through her oversized handbag, Faith said, 'I've got receipts and confirmations here—printed them out at the business centre. Do you want them as we go along, or shall I put them together in a full report at the end of the week?'

Dominic let his shoulders relax. 'It can wait. Just give me the full accounting when we're done. Including your hours and salary.'

Her eyes widened again as she looked at him. 'Okay. Will do.'

What was it that made it so hard for her to let people trust her? he wondered. Was it just that the scope of this job was a little outside her normal remit? Or was it something more?

Maybe he'd ask her, one day. If he got the chance.

'So, is it time for me to know where we're going yet?'

Faith gave him a mysterious smile. 'Soon,' she promised.

The Americans obviously hadn't been given any hints, either. They arrived in the lobby in dribs and drabs, dressed in the same cautious smart/casual attire Dominic had opted for. As soon as they were all assembled, Faith clapped her hands to get everyone's attention and said, 'Okay, ladies and gentlemen. Time for your first, proper London experience of the trip.'

Leading them out of the lobby, she kept talking. 'I know you've all been to London before, and I know that you've probably experienced a lot of the standard tourist attractions. But there are some things that are so quintessentially London, it would be wrong to miss them out this week. I promise there'll be some more unusual outings in your future but, just for tonight, I went for the classics.'

She certainly had. Dominic blinked at the sight of an old-fashioned Routemaster double-decker bus parked outside the Greyfriars Hotel. It looked utterly incongruous, like a penguin in the desert. Glancing over at Faith, he saw she was biting her lip, nervously awaiting his reaction. The Americans were already jostling to get on board, chattering and joking excitedly. But she was waiting to see what *he* thought. His opinion mattered to her. He liked that.

'Can't wait to see where it's taking us,' he said, and offered her his arm.

Grinning, she took it, tucking her hand into the crook of his elbow, and he realised that it must be the first time they'd touched. Because if he'd felt that electric shock at contact before, he'd have remembered. The touch, the scent, the closeness of her filled his senses, and he had to concentrate on putting one foot in front of the other to reach the bus and help her up the steps.

Note to self, he thought as he followed her. *Do not touch Faith Fowler again. That way lies madness.*

Faith held her breath as she stepped onto the bus, praying it was everything Julian had promised. She'd called in favours from every person she knew in the tourist trade in London to find the best options for the week ahead, and sent up thankful prayers when Julian told her that his latest venture, Big Red Tours, had a last-minute cancellation for that night. The photos and testimonials had been great, but you never knew for sure until you were there…

With the last step, she looked around and let out a relieved sigh. It was perfect.

Ben and Jerry were already seated at the table at the back, and a waiter in black tie dress was offering them a drink. The original bus seats had been torn out, replaced by wooden tables for two and four, bolted to the ground, as were the mismatched chairs around them. Red, white and blue cotton bunting hung from the ceiling, and the adverts were all replaced by vintage wartime posters.

Terri and Marie ventured upstairs and Faith followed, wondering at the sight of more bunting and an honest-to-God rooftop garden, with more seating areas dotted about.

'This is incredible, Faith!' Marie said, beaming as she took a glass of champagne from the upstairs waiter. 'Where on earth did you find such a thing?'

Faith smiled. 'Trade secret.'

She waited until everyone had explored the bus and chosen a seat before instructing the driver to start the tour. Period music, the sort that would have played on the American bases during the war, sang out from the speakers as they drove along the river, through the heart of London. The waiters served canapés and topped up champagne flutes as they went, the lights of the city sparkling outside the windows.

And all Faith could focus on was the fact that Dominic was sitting opposite her, smiling.

'Do I want to know how much this is costing me?' he asked, holding out his glass for a refill.

Faith shrugged. 'They had a last-minute cancellation, so I got a good deal.'

'I had no idea you could do this sort of thing. I mean, in general, not you personally.'

Quite honestly, Faith hadn't been sure of either. But, since everything seemed to be going okay, she decided not to mention it.

'The guy who started up the business—Julian—used to work with me last time I was doing tours in London. I thought it might be a fun start to the trip.'

'It is,' Dominic said, and he sounded as if he meant it. Faith felt something inside her start to relax and she reached for a glass of champagne.

'I just hope the next part of the evening is as big a success.'

'What is next?' Dominic asked.

Faith smiled. 'Dinner.'

Dinner, it turned out, was a bit of an understatement. Dominic hadn't known you could have canapés and champagne and roof gardens on buses, but he also hadn't realised you could actually eat dinner on Tower Bridge. Or, rather, inside it.

'Has this always been here?' he asked, staring out over the River Thames.

'They opened it for catering years ago,' Faith told him. 'We got lucky with a spare table tonight.'

They'd been getting lucky a lot, it seemed to Dominic. 'Another last-minute cancellation?'

Faith squirmed a little. 'Not exactly.'

Dominic raised an eyebrow. 'Let me guess; you used my name?'

'Wouldn't you?' Faith asked. 'To get a table at a restaurant, or a better seat on a flight, or tickets to some play?'

He wouldn't, but he couldn't deny that Shelley sometimes did. It just made him feel a little uncomfortable. 'I suppose. So, what happens to the poor saps we kicked out of this place tonight?'

Faith shook her head. 'I wouldn't do that. I just… persuaded them to rearrange things a little. That's all.'

'Can you talk anyone into anything?' he asked. After all, she'd done all this over the phone in the course of an afternoon. He couldn't even blame the mind-boggling effects of touching her, or even just looking at her, for the world falling at her feet. Or was that just him? Was everyone else immune, and it was just Dominic Beresford who found himself handing over jobs, money, credit cards and trust to this woman without a second thought?

Faith gave him a rueful smile. 'I wish I could. Do you know how many places I had to call, how many people I had to talk to, and how much research I put in to pulling all this together? A lot of places just said no upfront. Some I'm still in negotiations with to fit us in later in the week. I lucked out tonight, but I've still got a lot of hard work to put in to pull off the rest of the trip.'

She stopped, as if she hadn't meant to say so much.

'I'm sorry,' he said. 'I didn't mean to suggest you hadn't been working hard.'

'That's okay.' Faith's gaze darted away, out of the window. 'I mean, it's supposed to look effortless, isn't it? That old swan metaphor. Swimming smoothly along, paddling like mad underneath.'

Ridiculously, all he could think of at her words was Faith in a bikini. He cleared his throat, buying time for the image to dissipate. 'Well, it all seems like, uh, very smooth swimming so far.'

She gave him a curious look. 'Good. I'm glad you're enjoying it.' She glanced over his shoulder. 'Looks like our table's ready. I'd better gather the others from the bar.'

She strode off towards the Americans, who were all ordering cocktails. Apparently the champagne had put them in an excellent mood. If only he could get them to sign the contracts now…except that would be unethical. And his lawyers would kill him.

Sighing, Dominic headed for the large round table directly overlooking the river. Usually this sort of an evening was nothing but a chore, time away from the office he could ill afford. But Faith had managed to make it fun, different.

He couldn't wait to see what she had planned for the rest of the week.

CHAPTER SIX

IT WAS NEARLY midnight by the time the group climbed onto the Routemaster bus again and headed back to the hotel. And as they pulled up outside the Greyfriars, Faith silently thanked Dominic for quashing Henry's suggestion that they carry on to a club after dinner. She needed sleep and, before that, she needed to check her emails and reply to any confirming spaces for events over the next few days. And, as Dominic had pointed out, the Americans had a lot of meetings to fit in before their trip to the Beresford country estate later in the week. He needed them alert in the morning.

Fortunately, everyone except Henry had agreed. And when she'd promised to take him dancing another night—something else to add to her never-ending list of requests—even he'd been mostly appeased.

As the others headed for the lifts, waving tiredly behind them, Faith hung back with Dominic.

'Bed?' he asked, and for one moment, before she remembered that this was Dominic Beresford, more automaton than man, she thought he meant together and her eyes widened.

He noticed. Damned observant man. 'Are you going to yours now, I meant,' he said, not looking at all flustered at the misunderstanding. 'Rather than any sort of inappropriate proposition.'

'I knew that,' Faith said quickly. 'And yes. Bed. After I finish up some emails and such.'

Dominic nodded. 'Come on. We can work in the office of my suite. Keep each other awake while we finish up for the day. I've got some things I need to go over with you, anyway.'

She shouldn't. All she really wanted to do was take off her make-up, curl up in her bed with the late-night TV on low, and answer her emails until she passed out from exhaustion. Working in Dominic's room meant keeping on her high heels and actually making coherent conversation, both of which seemed like they might be beyond her until she'd got some sleep.

And yet…

'We can have a nightcap,' he said, striding off in the direction of the lift. 'Come on.'

She followed. He was her boss, after all, and she was obliged to bow to his requests. At least, that was what she was telling herself. She was too tired to think about the part of her that wasn't ready to say goodnight to him just yet.

Dominic's suite was twice the size of her, already impressive, accommodation. It had a kitchen area, a full dining table, a lounge filled with an oversized corner sofa and a glass coffee table and, tucked away in a corner by the bedroom door, the office.

There was only one desk, but two chairs, and another low table between them. Dominic took the desk chair, flipping open his laptop as he sat, so Faith settled into the visitor's chair—lower, more comfortable, and far too likely to send her to sleep.

Wearily, she reached into her bag for her tablet, contemplating just kicking her shoes off regardless. It was late. He'd understand. And her feet couldn't smell that much, could they?

Hmm. Maybe better not to risk it.

'Drink?' Dominic asked, and when she looked up she saw that he'd taken off his jacket, his shirt collar lying open beneath it. Her gaze fixed on the hollow at his neck, just above his collarbone, and she wondered, in what could only be a sleep-deprived daze, what it would be like to kiss him there. How his skin would feel under her lips, under her fingertips. 'I've got brandy, whisky, probably some rum…'

Faith blinked, and brought her attention back to the real world. 'Um, a whisky would be great. Thanks.'

Work. She was here to work. She really had to remember that.

She swiped a finger across the screen to bring it to life, and brought up her email program. Thirty-seven new emails. And since this was a new account Dominic had set up for her to do the job at hand, chances were that very few of them were spam. She suppressed a groan. She was never going to get to sleep tonight.

Dominic returned from the bar in the kitchen area with two tumblers, filled with ice and topped with what she imagined would probably be the finest whisky. Did she even remember what that tasted like? she wondered. Her father had only ever drunk the best, most expensive Scotch whiskies, and he'd tried to ensure that she grew up with a taste for the finer things, too.

'Here.' Dominic bent down to hand her the glass, and Faith's mouth moistened as that hollow at his neck grew closer.

This was ridiculous. She needed to go to bed.

As soon as she'd finished work.

Leaning back in the swivel chair at the desk, Dominic stretched his legs out in front of him, arms folded across his chest, and studied her.

'What?' Faith asked after a few long moments of scrutiny.

'You did a really great job tonight,' he said.

A warm glow flushed across her skin. 'Thank you. I knew it was important to you that your clients start the trip off with a bang.'

'And you certainly did that. The bus was a masterstroke.' And yet still he kept staring at her.

'Is there a *But...* here?' Faith didn't care if she was being blunt. It was far too late at night for subtle.

Dominic shook his head, unfolding his arms to push himself up into a straighter seated position. 'No buts. Just a few questions.'

Questions. Possibly her least favourite things. 'Such as?'

'Well, I never got to see your full résumé. We didn't even have a proper interview.'

'And you want to do that now?' Was the man crazy? 'You realise I'm already doing the job, right? And doing it well, according to you.'

'I know.' Dominic sounded completely unruffled. 'Like I say, I just want to know a little bit about your background.'

Her work background, Faith reminded herself, as her heart started to beat double time. All Dominic cared about was the job he'd hired her to do. Even if he did start developing suspicions about who she really was, he probably wouldn't care unless it interfered with one of his meetings. All she needed to do was keep things professional. How hard could that be?

'Well, I started working in events in London,' she

said, carefully editing out that part about how, as Lady Faith Fowlmere, she'd mostly been attending the events. Or, at most, throwing epic parties at her famous friends' houses. 'Then moved more into the tour guide side of things for a while.' After she ran away from home and became Faith Fowler. 'That's where I met my previous employer, who hired me to run his tours in Italy, where I've been for the last year and a half.' After Great-Uncle Nigel spotted her at an event in London and almost dragged her home and she realised that another country would be much easier to hide in. 'That's about it,' she finished with a shrug.

Dominic gazed at her, his eyes still assessing. But finally he nodded. 'Well, you obviously learned a lot in your time. Like I said, you're doing a great job. I trust you'll find more wonderful experiences to entertain us over the next few days. And you're coming to Beresford Hall with us later in the week, of course?'

Faith froze, the pleased smile she'd had at his words fixing into place as she realised what he was asking. Beresford Hall. Family seat. Full of people who knew the aristocracy, knew the families, kept up with the news.

Full of people who might recognise her.

'Actually, I was thinking that perhaps I should stay here and get the last couple of nights' entertainment sorted out?'

Dominic raised his eyebrows. 'We have Wi-Fi at the Hall these days, you know. You can work there.'

'Right. Of course.' Maybe she could hide on the bus. Or in a deserted corner bedroom. Or a cupboard. Anywhere. 'Only, I was thinking—' she started, but Dominic spoke over her.

'Then that's settled.' He tilted his head as he studied her. 'I'll be interested to see what you make of the old place.'

'Oh?' What did it matter what she thought? She was only the hired help.

But Dominic nodded. 'I want Beresford Hall to be an all-inclusive events location. It's more than a piece of history now, more than heritage. There are a lot of opportunities there—at our conference facility for a start. If you wanted me to introduce you to the head of events there…'

'No,' Faith said, too loudly. 'I mean, thank you. But really, this job is just a one-off. In between tours, like I said. I'm not looking for a permanent conference and events job here in the UK.' Especially not at Beresford Hall, where someone was bound to recognise her on her first day. No, thank you.

'So you'll be going back to Italy, after this week?' Dominic's gaze was sharp, and Faith got the impression that this was the real question he'd wanted to ask all along.

'Um, probably not Italy, no,' she admitted.

'So, you don't actually have another job lined up there?'

'Not exactly.' Faith plastered on a sparkling smile. 'I like to keep moving, you see. Don't want to be tied down to just one country.'

'I see.' Dominic leant back in his chair again. 'You never did tell me exactly why you had to leave Italy.'

Because my ex-boyfriend was threatening to bring the international media down on me, and the company I was working for went bust.

Neither of those facts were really going to put Dominic's mind at rest, were they? When in doubt, lie and run.

Faith gave a high, tinkling laugh. 'Well, you know,

after a while even pizza gets a bit boring. Besides, I wasn't sure my hips could take any more pasta!'

Before he had a chance to respond, Faith gathered up her tablet and notebook and shoved them into her bag.

'And I know how lucky I am to have this great job,' she added, getting to her feet. 'Which is why I need to get some sleep, ready to do my best work again tomorrow. Goodnight!'

She kept smiling until the door closed behind her, well aware that Dominic was still staring after her. But her heart didn't stop racing until she was back in her room.

She needed to make sure that Dominic didn't have any more chances to ask her questions about her previous life. It was far too tempting to tell him the truth.

She was lying to him, Dominic thought for the hundredth time as he took his seat on the executive coach taking the group to Beresford Hall three days later. Faith had been the perfect employee so far, arranging dinners and tours with such finesse that Dominic would have felt entirely comfortable letting her take charge of everything alone, except for one thing: he knew she was lying to him.

He had absolutely no idea why, but Dominic hadn't got where he was without developing the ability to spot when he was being lied to. The only question was, what on earth could Faith Fowler have to lie about?

Even if her career history had been embellished—although, given how little she'd actually told him, it seemed unlikely—she was doing a good enough job that he wouldn't care. She clearly didn't want to visit Beresford Hall—she'd come up with half a dozen excuses over the past few days to try and get out of it. But he'd stayed firm. He wanted her there, if only to find out why she didn't want to go. But it still didn't seem like something to lie about. Which meant it had to be something to do with why she was in such a hurry to leave Italy.

The last of his clients climbed aboard and took their seats, followed by Faith, in full professional mode. Shading her eyes from the sun streaming in through the coach window, she did a quick head count and nodded to the driver, barely sparing a glance and a tight smile for Dominic as she chose her own seat—as far away from his as was possible in the circumstances.

He'd lain awake for far too long after she'd left the other night, dreaming up elaborate falsehoods and scandalous pasts she could be hiding. Associations with the Mafia, drug trafficking, murder. Just the fact he was having to think about these things meant he should probably fire her and minimise whatever risk her lies represented.

But he didn't. Partly because he couldn't believe it was actually that bad. But mostly because she was Faith, and he wanted to give her a chance. He wanted her to stick around.

Which didn't mean he was going to stop trying to find out what she was hiding.

Beresford Hall lay less than two hours' drive outside London. Dominic spent the journey catching up on some reading, chatting with Ben, Henry and Marie about his next trip over to the States, and trying not to stare at the back of Faith's seat.

It was just the mystery, he told himself. Strange woman walks into his life, just when he needs her, and proceeds to do a perfectly good job while lying to him the whole time. Of course he was intrigued. Of course he'd been thinking about her. He needed to know the truth to protect himself, even if he suspected it would turn out to be nothing. A row with a boyfriend, perhaps. Nothing more.

And, whatever her reasons for leaving Italy, she didn't want to come to Beresford Hall either, that much was clear. But maybe she'd open up to him there. Maybe he could get her to talk.

Seeing the estate he'd saved from ruin and built up into a multi-million-pound business often made women feel fondly towards him. No reason to suppose a little imposing grandeur wouldn't do the same for Faith.

The coach pulled up the long driveway, curving through the landscaped gardens, past the fountains and up to the front of the Hall. In the past, all you'd have seen from the road was woodlands and immaculately trimmed hedges. These days, Dominic got a thrill from spotting a gang of archers heading off to the archery range, and a group of men in suits making their way towards the conference facilities. No weddings today, he supposed, with it being a Wednesday, but there were at least two stag dos booked in for the weekend, taking over the rally track and go-carting on the outer edges of the estate.

Dominic didn't try to dampen down the surge of pride he always felt when he saw the Hall, and especially when he saw the reaction of his clients to the magnificent building. Yes, he'd been born into a privileged family. But it had taken every ounce of his own determination and ability to make his family name, and estate, what it was today.

Maybe the people looking on only saw the money made, the clever business decisions he'd taken. But he, at least, knew that it was more than that. He'd done his time feeling ashamed as a boy—of his mother, his name, his life. But he'd grown up since then. He'd taken on the challenge and surpassed it. He'd reclaimed his heritage, his self-respect, his future.

And he had every right to be proud of that.

But when he finally caught Faith's eye, as she stood to guide everyone back off the bus, he didn't see the expected awe or appreciation in her gaze. Instead, she was frowning at the Hall as if it personally offended her.

His most likely reason for her reluctance to come with them that day rose up in the back of his mind again. Perhaps she just resented the aristocracy, and perceived privilege. Hadn't she been happy enough to use his name to get what she wanted from their suppliers that week, though? If there was one thing he couldn't stand, it was a hypocrite.

Dominic clenched a fist against the back of the seat beside him as he stood. He'd make sure Faith Fowler got a full tour of Beresford Hall. He wanted her to understand exactly what he'd achieved here, although he couldn't have said why it mattered to him so much.

Beresford Hall was beautiful, magnificent, a shining example of some sort of architecture or another, and everything else the guidebook said it would be. But all Faith could see was the shadow of Fowlmere Manor hanging over it, reminding her how hard she'd worked to get away from places like this. People like this.

Sure, Fowlmere was maybe half the size of Beresford Hall, and there were far fewer people hanging around it these days, but the similarities caught her everywhere she turned, and she couldn't shake the shiver that crept over her shoulders when she thought how close she'd come to being trapped somewhere like this her whole life.

Dominic led them up the stone steps to the imposing front doors, hauling them open and holding one to let them pass into the main hall. It was early on a weekday, but there had been several coaches parked in the car park when they arrived and the hall already boasted three lines for tickets. This, Faith supposed, was where Fowlmere really differed. Even if her father had let them, what tourists would want to pay to visit a crumbling manor that had sold most of its heirlooms to pay gambling debts?

Beresford Hall was often held up as an example of heritage done right. Open most days to the public, save one wing that was kept as family quarters, Dominic had put history on display for all to share and he'd done it in style.

'Come on through, guys,' he said, lifting a red tasselled rope to let them skip the queue. 'I'll give you the house tour myself, before we get a better look at the newer additions to the property.'

Faith followed, remembering the horrible attempts to open Fowlmere to the public when she was a child. Only two days a year, her father had decreed, and he'd give the tours himself. Except, when it came down to it, it turned out he didn't know much about the history of the house, or the family. And when her mother had stepped in to take over, Faith had realised she was already slurring her words at ten in the morning.

Faith had learned everything she could about the Manor and her ancestry, to be ready for the next open day. But, in the end, her father had declared it a waste of time and shut the gates again.

Not so at Beresford Hall.

'This is the chamber prepared for Queen Victoria, when she visited the Hall.' Dominic waited as they all took in the room, with its rich red walls and imposing four-poster bed. Gold accents glittered on everything, adding a shine to the faded history. 'Beresford Hall has been host to five British monarchs, and we have memorabilia from each of their visits.'

He was obviously proud of his family and his history, Faith thought. She wondered what that would be like. Whether she'd have stayed if her own family hadn't been such a shambles. Who would she be if she'd grown up somewhere like Beresford, where her future was neatly mapped out for success, rather than finding buckets to catch drips from leaking roofs, or hiding bottles from her mother and lying to debt-collectors when they came looking for her father?

But she wasn't that girl. She was Faith Fowler now, and that was all she ever intended to be.

With a sigh for things lost, Faith followed Dominic through the next doorway to a magnificent dining room, staring out of the window instead of listening to him talk. She was his employee, not his girlfriend. She didn't have to hang on his every word. She didn't have to care about this house, or its history. She didn't have to learn which king stayed when.

Because this wasn't her world any more. And it never would be again.

CHAPTER SEVEN

'WHAT ARE YOU frowning at?' Sylvia asked.

Dominic looked down at his sister, taking in her wrinkled up nose and exasperated eyes, and tried very hard to shake his bad mood. 'Nothing. It's all perfect. Thanks for setting this up for me.'

Sylvia shrugged. 'Just an ordinary day's work. You do realise I do this for paying customers every day.'

It showed, Dominic thought. When they'd first opened the tea rooms in the old stables, he'd been doubtful. They already had the restaurant, over in the Orangery, offering fine dining to the visitors, and the café over on the other side of the yard, serving sandwiches and drinks. A third eating area seemed like overkill.

But Sylvia had wanted it. Sylvia, who never really asked for anything, only went along with his plans and said, 'If that's what we need to do.' So when she'd said, 'No, Dominic. You're wrong. This will be a really good thing,' he'd listened.

He was glad he had, now. Sylvia had taken on all the planning and running of the tea rooms, picking out the perfect curtains and matching tablecloths, light and airy without being too chintzy. She'd tasted every baker's cakes from Beresford to London, and finally hired a young man called Russell to bake the scones, cakes and biscuits for the afternoon teas. People flocked to them—not just the senior citizens on their day trips, which he'd sort of expected, but everyone. Hard-nosed businessmen on a break from their conference schedule over at the events suite. Lovers checking out the Hall as a possible wedding venue. Hungover stag parties. Everyone.

For once, Dominic was actually pleased to be proved wrong.

The Americans certainly seemed to be enjoying it, too. He'd originally asked Sylvia to find them a private room somewhere, but she'd refused, saying half the charm of the tea rooms was the atmosphere. And she'd been right again. They were chatting away with the tourists on the next table, exclaiming over the scones and clotted cream and the cucumber sandwiches.

Even Faith looked as if she might be enjoying herself for the first time that day.

'You're staring at her again,' Sylvia commented, and he could hear the smirk in her voice.

Diverting his gaze towards the tower of cakes on the counter, Dominic said, 'Staring at whom?'

'Your event planner. Tour guide. Kat's replacement. Whoever she is.'

'Merely a last-minute employee for the week,' Dominic said, ignoring the tiny part of his brain that screamed at him that she should be more. 'Kat cancelled on us.'

'Understandably.' She gave him a sideways look. 'After that video.'

Just hearing the words made the shame rise up again, stinging in his throat. The memory of the moment he'd first seen it sharp and constant in his brain. And the swift realisation that what hurt most wasn't the personal betrayal, wasn't the fact that Kat had slept with another man. It was the humiliation. The way it sent him right back to his childhood, and those unbearable days after his mother left, when all anybody seemed able to talk or write or think about was his family's shame.

He'd promised himself he'd never be in that position again, and Kat had made him break that promise. Maybe he couldn't have changed what happened with his mother, but he should have been able to control Kat. And he could sure as hell make sure it never happened again. Which meant finding out what Faith was hiding.

Sylvia was still watching him carefully, as if waiting to see if he might explode at the very mention of the video. Dominic closed his eyes and wished very hard he'd never heard of YouTube. 'Just tell me you haven't watched it.'

'I don't think there's a person we know that hasn't seen at least a glimpse of it.' Sylvia shook her head. 'You think you know a person.'

'It's wildly unsuitable and inappropriate for you to even mention it.'

'I don't know why you're so bothered. It's not like you're in it.' Dominic looked at her, and she winced. 'Of course, I suppose that might not actually make things any better.'

'I'd like to stop talking about this now, please.'

Sylvia gave a quick nod. 'Absolutely. Good idea. You can tell me about your latest employee instead.'

As if that was any safer a topic. 'What do you want to know?'

'Her name would be a good start. Where you met. What she's like. That kind of thing.'

'You realise you'll probably never see her again after today, right?'

'Oh, I don't know,' Sylvia said airily. 'At the very

least, there's the theatre trip you promised faithfully to let me come along on…'

Damn it. He'd forgotten that. He'd have to ask Faith to try and score an extra ticket.

'You forgot. Didn't you?'

'Of course not,' Dominic lied. 'I just need to ask Faith something…'

'Aha! So her name is Faith. We're getting somewhere.'

Dominic rolled his eyes. Apparently she wasn't giving up on this one any time soon. 'Her name is Faith Fowler, she's a tour guide I met in Italy and hired to come over and run this tour, and she doesn't like stately homes. That's about all I know.'

Sylvia's brow furrowed. 'Except this one. She likes this stately home. Don't you, Faith?'

Glancing up, Dominic saw Faith approaching, too late to steer her away from his sister's insatiable curiosity.

'I love these tea rooms,' Faith said, not really answering the question. 'And the scones are to die for.'

'I'll introduce you to Russell before you go,' Sylvia replied, suitably distracted. 'He's a marvel in the kitchen.'

'Faith, we're going to need an extra ticket for the theatre tomorrow,' Dominic said. For some reason, the idea of Faith and Sylvia getting chummy made him nervous.

'Not a problem.' Faith whipped out her tablet and made a note. 'We're in the box anyway, and I think there are a couple of extra seats at the very back. Or I can always just skip it.'

'No. I need you there.' The words came out too firm, even to Dominic's ears, and both women looked at him in surprise.

'I'll still be around to get you all there and home again,' Faith said.

'Still, you don't want to miss the play,' Sylvia said, but she was looking at Dominic. He tried to keep his face blank. The last thing he needed was his little sister questioning his motives for hiring Faith. And he didn't want to explain that he needed to keep Faith close until he discovered what secrets she was keeping.

'I'm not much of a theatre person,' Faith said with a tight smile.

She was lying again, Dominic thought, wondering when he'd got so adept at spotting even her little fibs. But why? Why wouldn't she want to go to the opening night of the play she'd been so excited to score them tickets for?

'Is this another wardrobe issue?' he guessed, and Sylvia started staring at him again.

Faith flushed, the pink colour clashing with her scarlet cardigan. 'Not entirely. I could always wear my black dress again.'

'You've worn that dress every evening this week,' he pointed out. 'It's going to fall apart if you dry clean it once more.'

Faith blinked at him. 'I didn't think you'd notice.'

'I didn't think he could tell one dress from another,' Sylvia added, glancing between them. 'It must be a very special dress.'

'It's really not,' Faith told her.

'So go buy a new one,' Dominic said. 'You can go shopping while we're in meetings tomorrow. Just put it on the card.'

'I really don't need—'

'I'll come with you!' Sylvia clapped her hands to-

gether with excitement. 'It'll be great! I'm in town anyway for that evening, and I love a good shopping trip…'

Faith glanced between them, and suddenly Dominic
felt just a little sorry for her. Not enough to get her out
of a shopping trip with his sister, though.

'Well, that would be…' Faith started.

'Expensive,' Dominic finished for her. 'That's the
word you're looking for. Expensive and exhausting.'

'Oh, shush,' Sylvia said. 'You want her to look her
best, don't you?'

He didn't care, Dominic realised. He didn't care what
she wore, what she looked like. He just wanted her there
with him. And not just so he could uncover her lies.

He was in trouble.

Faith spent the coach ride back to the hotel sulking.
Not that anyone could tell; she was cheery and chatty
enough to the clients. Maybe Dominic might have noticed but, since it was his fault anyway, she didn't care.

How had this happened? She'd known all along the
theatre trip was a risk, but not much more than anything
else she'd agreed to that week. The theatre was one of
her mother's passions; her circle of friends liked to pa-
tronise up-and-coming directors, playwrights, actors.
Tomorrow, the opening night of a well-hyped show, di-
rected by London's next big thing…no way they'd miss
it. Maybe her mum wouldn't be there, but someone who
would know Faith on sight would be, she had no doubt.

She'd planned on hiding out in the coach. She could
get them all in and settled easy enough, then slip out
and hide. Mum's gang were bound to be the last in so,
as long as she got the rest of them there early, she'd be
fine. When Dominic had said about needing a seat for

Sylvia, things got even easier. They'd never even notice she'd gone.

But now, suddenly, not only was she attending the
bloody thing, she was buying a new frock, just for the
occasion.

And the absolute worst thing was, she didn't even
mind. Because it meant an evening with Dominic,
dressed up and looking her best, and as close to off-
duty as she could get this week.

Faith sighed, and slouched down in her seat. Falling for her employer. How cliché. And just the sort of
man her mother would love her to marry, too. Perfect.

After the long day trip, Faith had planned a quiet
dinner at a restaurant not far from the hotel. With only
an hour to answer emails, catch up on work and get
changed for dinner, she didn't have much choice but
to pull on the hated black dress again. She'd thought
it was versatile enough to see her through the week,
but then she hadn't fully anticipated having to accompany the group on every single one of their evenings
out. And she hadn't counted on Dominic being there,
watching her, either.

Taking in her reflection in the hotel room mirror,
she pulled a face. And then she grabbed her red shoes,
red cardigan and brightest red lipstick. Worn right, he
might not even notice the dress underneath.

'Nice dress,' Dominic said ten minutes later when they
met in the lobby. Faith pulled a face at him, and he
laughed.

Dinner, Faith thought, would have been more or less
perfect if it wasn't for two things. One, the heel of her
shoe breaking as she returned from the bathrooms after

dessert. And two, Jerry insisting on accompanying her back to the hotel when she decided to leave while the others had coffee. After four days of fending off his advances, she was running out of excuses.

Even then, it might have been salvaged if Jerry hadn't followed her up to her room, staring intently down her cleavage as she rooted through her bag for her keycard.

'Thanks for helping me home,' she said, smiling falsely up at him. 'I think I can manage from here.' She waved her keycard, just to prove the point.

'What kind of a gentleman would I be if I didn't see you safely into your room?' He gave her a smile that made her want to shudder. 'I can check for monsters under your bed, if you like.'

I'm much more concerned about what you want to do in *my bed.* 'I'm a big girl now, Jerry. I think I can manage.'

His gaze dropped down to her breasts again. 'You certainly are.'

Okay, that was enough. 'Jerry, I'm tired. I'm going to bed. I suggest you do the same.' How much wine had he drunk with dinner? His eyes weren't entirely focused when he finally managed to look up at her face.

'Aw, come on. Just a quick nightcap. After all, we missed out on after-dinner drinks.'

'I really don't think that's a good idea,' Faith said, slipping her keycard into the door. 'Early start and all tomorrow. Goodnight, Jerry.'

A hand appeared above hers on the door, pushing it open, and the first pangs of panic stabbed in Faith's chest. Focusing on her breathing, she grabbed the handle and yanked it closed again, almost catching Jerry's fingers in the door as she did so.

'I said goodnight, Jerry.' The words came out much

calmer than she felt. Her heart pounded against her rib-cage and she wanted to kick out, stamp on his feet in her one remaining red heel, the way the self-defence classes had taught her.

But he was Dominic's client. And he hadn't actually done anything yet, except make her feel desperately uncomfortable.

Of course, if his hands moved from the door to her body, she was taking him down.

Fingers, hot and sweaty, landed on her hip and Faith didn't waste time thinking any more. Stamping down with her right foot, she tried not to smile in satisfaction as Jerry let go and howled.

'Oh, I'm so sorry. Was that your foot?' she asked, her voice syrupy sweet.

'You bitch! You wait until I tell your boss about this.' Jerry was practically curled up over his foot, his face shining red, his eyes furious.

Faith managed one moment of relief before a figure appeared at the edge of her vision, coming around the corridor from the lift. And, before she could even look, she heard Dominic say, 'Tell her boss about what?' and her heart plummeted.

CHAPTER EIGHT

JERRY HAD SCAMPERED back to his room before Dominic could get any coherent account of what had happened, which he supposed meant he'd have to trust Faith's version of the story to be fully accurate. Normally, he hated only hearing one side. But on this occasion…he trusted Faith a hell of a lot more than the man he'd been doing business with for nearly three years.

'Tell me what happened,' he said as Faith let them both into her room, kicked off her ruined shoes and headed straight for the minibar.

'Pretty much exactly what you think happened.' She pulled out a small bottle of Scotch and reached for the glasses on the counter above.

'I don't know what happened,' he said reasonably as he took a seat in the armchair. 'All I saw was my client on the floor, practically crying in pain.'

Faith shrugged. 'I stood on his foot.'

Dominic's gaze dropped to the ridiculously high heels she'd discarded in the corner. The one with the intact heel certainly looked as if it could do some damage. 'Why?'

'Would you believe me if I said it was an accident?' Faith poured the whisky evenly between the two glasses and handed one to him.

'No,' he said, taking a sip. Not as good as his, but not bad.

With a sigh, Faith dropped onto the sofa, curling her legs up under her. 'He was drunk. He got…ideas. And he didn't appear able to comprehend the word *no*.'

Dominic stopped, stared, his blood heating up. He'd kill him. How could he even think for a moment that Faith—Faith!—would want to…?

'You don't believe me.' Glancing over, he saw Faith's wide eyes looking at him with disappointment.

'Oh I believe you,' he said, the words scratchy in his throat. 'And that bastard is on the next flight home.' Pushing himself to his feet, he let his anger carry him towards the door, but Faith stopped him before he got there, her small hand on his arm, a touch he hadn't expected.

'He was drunk,' she repeated. 'And stupid. Very, very stupid. But I took care of it.'

'You shouldn't have had to.'

'No, I shouldn't. But, trust me, it's not the first time it's happened. Guys get ideas in hotels, for some reason. But I learnt to look after myself, and no one has ever got any further than a hand on my waist unless I wanted them to, I promise.'

She sounded so calm, so certain, that Dominic's blood started to cool, just a little. 'I still want to punish him.'

'Oh, by all means,' Faith said, giving him a lopsided smile. 'Just find something more subtle than getting yourself arrested for grievous bodily harm, yeah?'

Dropping back down onto the couch, Dominic realised that he would have done. He'd have gone to that bastard's room and pounded him to a pulp, without caring what the police would do, or what the press would say, what damage it would do to the business, to these negotiations. Three years of strategising down the drain, and the Beresford name on the front of every paper for all the wrong reasons again.

He couldn't risk that.

He wanted to believe that he'd have done it anyway because he was a noble man who knew right from wrong. But, as Faith sat down beside him, her thigh close enough to touch his, he knew that gentlemanly behaviour had nothing to do with it.

He'd have hurt that man for touching Faith. Any other woman...he'd have reported it to Jerry's superiors, to the police if it had gone far enough. But Faith... was different.

'You okay?' she asked, bumping her arm against his.

He gave a humourless laugh. 'Shouldn't I be asking you that?'

'Probably. But I'm clearly fine.'

Dominic studied her, taking in her pale skin, and the spots of pink on her cheeks that were probably the fault of the whisky. 'Are you?'

She gave a half-shrug, and took another sip. 'Just a little shaken. I should have known better than to let him walk me back, really.'

'This is in no way your fault,' Dominic said firmly.

'Oh, I know that. Trust me, I blame him entirely.'

'Good.' Leaning back against the sofa, Dominic began to imagine ways of making Jerry pay. At the very least, he was going to get every meeting request for every video conference until the end of time, whether he needed to be there or not.

'You're thinking of torture techniques, aren't you?' Faith curled her feet up under her again, twisting to face him on the sofa, and he couldn't help but notice the way

the skirt of that bloody black dress rode up her thighs.
God, he was as bad as Jerry.

'Corporate torture,' he promised. 'Entirely legal.'

'Well, that's okay then. Wouldn't want my boss getting into trouble.'

Her boss. Of course that was all he was to her. And
he wouldn't even be that much longer. Once the Americans were on the plane home, she'd be gone. Onto the
next job, the next adventure. He couldn't even plan on
calling her back next time he had guests in town; God
only knew where she'd be by then.

Unless…

'I meant to talk to you about that, actually.' Or he
would have, if he'd thought of it before now.

Faith's eyebrows drew together. 'About what?'

Dominic took a deep breath, and made his play.
'About whether you'd like to make the boss thing a
more permanent arrangement.'

Faith stared at him long enough that he started to go
out of focus, then snapped her gaze away. Of course
he was so impressed by her professional abilities that
he wanted to keep her around. Nothing to do with her
more personal attributes. She had to remember that.

But still…he did want to keep her around. Just the
idea gave her a warm glow greater than anything she'd
got from the alcohol in her glass.

Except, she couldn't stay. The realisation made her
wince into her whisky as she looked down so she didn't
have to see his face as she answered.

'That's…very kind…' She scouted around her poor
scrambled brain to find the right words, but Dominic
was already talking again before she got to them.

'It makes sense, right? I mean, I need a new tour

company, one way or another, and I got to thinking that it would be easier if I just had someone on staff to take care of these things. Obviously we'd need to come to a more formal arrangement—you'd need an office in my building, and we'd have to discuss salary, relocation expenses and all of that.'

She wanted to say yes. It was a fantastic offer, something that would really let her build up her life as Faith Fowler. But how could she do it in the shadow of her family name? How could she risk living in London again, knowing that any moment they could find her and thrust her back into the limelight?

Dominic gave her an encouraging smile and she tried to return it.

Would it really be so bad, even if they did find her? She was a grown woman. They couldn't make her go home. And with a stable job with Dominic, she'd never be reliant on them for money, or anything else again. This could be her chance at true independence.

Until Dominic found out the truth. No way he'd hang onto an employee who brought the paparazzi down on him for harbouring a missing heiress. And once they'd found her, all the stories would start up again, and the pictures of her leaving that damn hotel room would be back in circulation, and the rumours about her relationship with a married drug addict rock star...no. Dominic wouldn't stand for any of that. Even if she could make him believe that the papers had it all wrong.

No. She couldn't stay. There was no place for her in Dominic's world any more, if there ever really had been. Getting close to Dominic...it was a mistake. One she was very afraid she might have already made. But there had to be a line, a point she couldn't cross. She couldn't fall in love. And so she couldn't risk staying.

Besides, she told herself, she didn't want to stay in London anyway. She wanted to see more of the world, more than just Italy.

Even if she'd rather see more of Dominic.

'You're going to say no, aren't you?'

Faith gave him an apologetic smile, and he shook his head.

'Is this because of the Lord thing?'

She blinked. 'The Lord thing?'

Shifting to face her, Dominic's expression was serious. 'Yeah. I saw the way you were at Beresford Hall today. You hated every minute of it. So, what's the problem? You hate the aristocracy?'

I was the aristocracy. 'Of course not.'

'So, what, then? Trust me, whatever it is, I've heard it before. That I'm an over-privileged, spoilt brat who only got where I am because of my family. That I'm stealing from the mouths of others by having so much. That—'

'Dominic.' Faith spoke as calmly as she could, placing her hand against his arm again. 'I didn't say any of those things.'

He sighed. 'But you did hate being there today.'

No point lying about that one. 'Yeah.'

'So, why?'

Faith drew in a deep breath while she considered her answer. Obviously she couldn't tell him the truth—that it reminded her too much of her own home. But he clearly wasn't going to be fobbed off with a blatant lie, either. Besides, even if she couldn't stay, she wanted him to think well of her when she was gone.

'I guess I…I don't know how to explain it, really. It made me feel uncomfortable. All that history and opulence.'

Dominic frowned. 'Uncomfortable? Why? I mean,

I've had people be angry about the privilege, had people be jealous or bitter. But why uncomfortable?'

'Does it really matter?'

'It does to me.'

He was very close now, closer than even Jerry had been before she maimed him. When had she shifted so close? When had the hand on his arm become a gentle caress rather than a calming gesture? When had his thigh pressed so closely against her legs, his arm along the back of the sofa just behind her?

She didn't ask why it mattered to him; it was enough that it did. And she wanted him to know the truth, to have one moment of honesty from her before she left, taking all her lies and secrets with her.

'It made me feel trapped. Like all that history, tradition, expectation were weighing down on me, instead of you. Like there was no room for you to be yourself or explore what you wanted. Because the family name, upholding what that means, would always make you follow a certain course. That's why it made me uncomfortable.'

Dominic stared at her, realising too late that he was close enough now to see every fleck of green and brown in her hazel eyes. He could kiss her without moving more than a few centimetres.

But he wouldn't. Because of Jerry, because she was leaving, and because the very basis of his life made her 'uncomfortable'.

'That's not how it is.' Sitting back, he slid his arm back along the sofa, tucking his elbow in at his side, keeping his hands far away from her tempting skin. 'What I've done at Beresford Hall...that's all me. When my father died, he left things in a less than ideal condition.' Had she ever heard the story? he wondered. Everyone he met in society knew; he could see it in their eyes when he was introduced. After all, it was such a good story—the Lady of the Manor who went wild, running off to the Med with a billionaire tycoon, leaving behind two children and a distraught husband. A husband who barely got over the loss enough to look after the children, let alone the estate. Who could blame people for telling it over and over again?

Of course, they didn't see beyond the pictures in the society pages. His mother, living it up on some yacht, flaunting her adultery, her betrayal. And his mother never had to see what it did to the family she left behind. How Sylvia cried and screamed and then went silent for two long months. How the husband she left behind faded to a shadow of a man.

Or how Dominic dealt, every day, with the photographers and the journalists, at the door and on the phone. And with the constant humiliation of every single person in his life knowing how little he meant to his own mother.

It came up less in the business world, at least—one reason he preferred to keep his focus on building up the business and the brand, rather than attending the compulsory charity galas and events that he'd inherited with the title. But did ordinary people really care? Did Faith?

She raised her eyebrows at him. 'Less than ideal? What does that mean?'

Did it matter any more? The shame he burned with at the memories? Had he done enough, finally, to set it all behind him? Would he ever?

Faith was still waiting for an answer, though. He swallowed down the last gulp of his whisky, enjoying the slight burn in his throat. 'After my mother left…my father checked out of life,' he said bluntly. 'He didn't care about anything any more. Not even the scandal my mother left behind. The estate suffered.' He shrugged. 'When he died, he left us with nothing but our name.'

'And you fought back from that.' Faith's eyes were wide as she watched him. 'You built up the estate, the business…'

'I saved the family name,' he corrected her. 'The rest was incidental.'

'It meant that much to you. The name, I mean.'

'Yes.' He glanced away. 'It was all I had left, after all.'

She was silent for a long moment, but when he looked back her gaze was still fixed on him. Her teeth bit down on her lip, a flash of white in the dim lamplight of the darkening hotel room, and he wondered what it was she wanted to say. And whether she'd decide to say it.

'My father,' she said finally. 'He was—is—the world's most charming man. But…he gambled. Still does, I imagine. He…lost. A lot. Even if he'd never admit it. Life had to go on as if everything was normal, like we were as good as—better than—everyone else. Even if we couldn't afford to buy my school uniform. That's one of the reasons I moved away. I didn't want to watch him destroy himself, or our family.'

The words caught him in the chest, and it took him a moment to identify why. That was, he realised, the first real thing she'd ever told him about herself. He knew about the tours she'd led, the people she'd met. He knew her opinion on subjects as varied as clothes and theatre and London traffic.

And now he knew something of her. A small token, before she left him.

It wasn't enough.

'Didn't you ever want to just give up?' Faith asked. 'Just walk away from it all and start a new life?'

Had he? He couldn't remember. It had never seemed an option. From the moment he'd inherited the title, he knew exactly what he needed to do and he just got on with it. Besides... 'How could I? Sylvia was only ten, and we had nothing...I couldn't leave.'

Faith's smile was sad. 'No. No, of course you couldn't.'

Tipping the last drops of whisky down her throat, she placed her glass on the coffee table. Dominic stared at her lips and the way her tongue darted out to catch the last drop of liquid from them. He wanted to kiss her. And he knew, just knew, from the way she leant into him, close enough to touch, that she wouldn't pull away. She wouldn't say no, wouldn't pull any of her self-defence moves on him. She'd let him kiss her, and then what? He'd take her to bed, just to let her leave him in a few days' time? She wasn't going to stay. And he was already in too deep. He couldn't risk falling any further. Not after Kat.

'You never did tell me the real reason you left Italy,' he said. Maybe now she knew some of his secrets, his truths, she'd be willing to share some of her own. Let him in enough that he could stop worrying about her lies.

Faith pulled back, wrapping her arms around her knees. Suddenly, even though she still sat on the same sofa, she felt miles further away. How bad was her truth that she couldn't let it near him?

'That day we met, at the airport,' she said, her voice slow.

'I remember,' he said drily. As if he would ever forget.

'I'd just found out that the company I worked for had gone bankrupt. I got everyone in my tour group sorted out with flights and hotels but I...I was stranded. Until you offered me this job.'

'Until you demanded it, you mean.' She was telling the truth, he was sure. But he was equally certain that there was more, something she was still hiding.

'Hey, I'm doing a good job, aren't I?'

'You're doing an incredible job,' he said, and she looked up, wide eyes surprised. 'I just wish you'd stop lying to me and let me see the real you.' He got to his feet, ignoring her alarmed stare. 'You should get some sleep. Goodnight, Faith.'

CHAPTER NINE

'HOW ABOUT THIS one?' Sylvia asked, and Faith glanced up from the racks of overpriced, over-decorated dresses to shake her head at Dominic's sister for the tenth time that morning. And they were only on the second shop. Faith sighed. Dominic hadn't been kidding when he'd said this would be exhausting.

Sylvia hung the dress back on the rail with a clatter of metal on metal. 'You know, this would be a lot easier if you could tell me what you're looking for.'

Faith flicked past another few dresses. 'I told you, I'm not sure. I'll know it when I see it.'

'Utterly unhelpful.' Flinging herself into a cream leather armchair outside the fitting rooms, Sylvia pulled out a small pink suede notepad and a sparkly pen. 'Come on. Let's figure this out. First question: cocktail or ballgown?'

'Cocktail, definitely. No one wears floor-length to the theatre any more, do they?'

Sylvia shrugged her slim shoulders and made a note on the pad. 'Not anyone your age, anyway. Okay, black or colour?'

'Colour,' Faith replied. 'I'm sick to death of black after a week in that one dress.'

'Plain or decorated?'

'Plain. It'll go with more accessories that way.' If she was getting to buy a dress on Dominic's card, it might as well be something she could wear again and again.

She turned her attention back to the rack and was only half paying attention when Sylvia spoke again.

'Okay, most important question, then—how do you want my brother to look when he sees you in it?'

'Awed,' she said without thinking, then smacked a hand over her mouth. 'I didn't say that,' she muttered through her fingers.

Sylvia gave a gleeful grin. 'Oh, you did. You most certainly did.'

'Well, I shouldn't have.' Faith studied the dresses again with unwarranted attention, since they were all exactly what she didn't want, but did at least distract from the way her cheeks were burning. 'He's my boss.'

'Only for a few more days,' Sylvia pointed out.

'At which point I'll be leaving. Hardly a winning argument.'

'You could stay,' Sylvia suggested. 'Maybe Dominic could offer you a permanent job.'

'At which point he'd be my boss again.' Faith shook her head. 'Besides, he already did. I think he's much more interested in keeping me as an employee than anything else.'

'Given the way he was staring at you yesterday, I'd take that as a compliment,' Sylvia said, her tone dry. 'You must be incredibly good at your job.'

'I am.' Faith pushed the dresses back along the rail. 'Which is why we're going to try the next shop in the hope of finding a perfectly work appropriate dress for tonight, so I can go out and do what I'm being paid for. Nothing more, nothing less.'

'Are you sure?' Sylvia asked, holding the shop door

open for her. 'Because I have to tell you, Dominic never looked at Kat that way.'

Something froze inside her, and Faith was awfully afraid it might be her heart. Like it had been shocked into stillness by the idea that Dominic wanted her more than she'd ever dared to imagine.

He'd almost kissed her the night before; she'd seen it in his face. She still wasn't sure what had stopped him, although she could list a dozen perfectly reasonable options off the top of her head. Probably it was Jerry, she'd decided. Dominic would never try anything so soon after she'd had to fend off the attentions of another man. It wouldn't be Proper.

And Dominic was all about Proper.

Which was exactly why she couldn't let herself have him. She had given up any chance of a place in Dominic's world when she ran away, and that was a decision she had to stick by.

Besides, if they started something, anything real, the truth would come out. It always did. And she couldn't bear the thought of the disgust and disappointment on Dominic's face when he found out.

She ignored the small part of her brain that said she only had a few more days. Maybe she could have that, at least. Surely she could keep her secret that long…

It all came down to one simple fact. If Dominic knew who she really was, what she'd done, he wouldn't want her. And on the infinitesimally small off chance he did, if she wanted a real chance with Dominic, she'd never get to be Faith Fowler again.

Lose-lose.

Kind of like the shopping expedition so far.

She sighed as Sylvia dragged her into the next boutique, another tiny, expensive shop filled with incredible dresses Faith's mother would have loved.

'Do you really think we're going to find anything in here?' she asked.

'We won't know until we look,' Sylvia replied, already scouring through the individual dress hangers on the walls to find the perfect outfit.

Faith was pretty sure that not one of the dresses Sylvia was looking at would fit over her not exactly model-shaped frame. The women these dresses were intended for didn't have curves. She couldn't even swear they had hips, looking at the narrow cuts.

Still, Sylvia seemed happy browsing through the fabrics, so Faith let her attention wander, imagining what the evening ahead might be like if she did let herself be talked into some glamorous, fabulous dress that showcased all her best assets.

Would Dominic notice? Would he look her over in that way of his and take in her figure, rather than her inappropriate clothes? Would he sit beside her in the theatre, transfixed by the plunging neckline of her dress?

Probably not.

The bell over the shop door chimed and Faith looked up absently, then froze. Lady Ginny Gale. Her mother's best friend.

Her head felt fuzzy, as if every thought she'd ever had was buzzing in there, all at the same time. She couldn't let Ginny see her, recognise her. This was just what she'd been afraid would happen at the theatre that night.

Getting to her feet as casually as she could—jerky movements would only draw attention to her—Faith turned her body away from the door, where Ginny was talking to the assistant. Then, grabbing the first dress she came to, she murmured to Sylvia, 'I'm just going to try this on.'

Sylvia's eyebrows rose in surprise, probably because the dress was everything Faith had said she didn't want—full length, black and decorated with crystals in a fan pattern on the skirt—but Faith ignored her, moving serenely towards the safety of the fitting room.

Of course, once safely behind the heavy locked door, she collapsed onto the velvet padded seat and buried her head in her hands.

This was why she couldn't stay in London. This was why she couldn't consider trying to seduce Dominic that night. As if she needed the reminder. She wanted out of his world, not back in. She'd been crazy to even take the job, once she'd figured out who he was.

Still, she'd see it through now, of course. Which meant finding something utterly un-Faith-like to wear that night. She needed to be so unrecognisable even her own mother would walk past her in the lobby if she showed up. And she wasn't going to find that in any of the shops Sylvia was dragging her to.

'Faith? Are you okay?' Sylvia's voice rang through the fitting room, and Faith winced. Why hadn't she lied about her first name, too? Would have made things much easier. Except she'd always been Faith, and she hadn't wanted to lose that too, when she was letting go of everything else.

She'd probably forget to answer to another name, anyway.

'Fine,' she called back, her voice low. 'I don't think this is the one for me.'

'Well, I think we could have predicted that before you came in here,' Sylvia said drily. 'Lady Gale has left, by the way. She was just placing an order for a new jacket.'

Was she that obvious? 'Who?' Faith tried innocently but, as she unlocked the door to the changing room, Sylvia was standing on the other side, arms folded and eyebrows raised.

'Want to explain to me what just happened?' she asked.

Faith shook her head. 'Not really. It's old news now, anyway.' Which didn't mean anyone had forgotten about it. Certainly not the Internet.

'Former employer?' Sylvia guessed.

'Something like that.'

'I won't tell Dominic, you know. Not if you don't want me to.'

'There's nothing to tell,' Faith lied. Then, leaving the hideous black dress hanging on the rail, she headed back out into the shop and straight for the door. 'Come on; I think I've got a better idea of what I'm looking for now.'

Dominic was a busy man. He'd had important meetings all day, emails and calls to deal with, not to mention some valuable forward planning with Marie and Henry that afternoon. They'd made some real headway on the expansion plans, and Dominic could almost see his dreams coming to life.

Which was why it was particularly embarrassing to admit, even to himself, that he'd spent most of the day wondering what sort of a dress Sylvia would persuade Faith to buy for the theatre that evening.

He hadn't had a chance to see Faith all day, despite his attempt to catch her at breakfast. He had, however, seen Jerry, which had been entertaining enough in itself.

The man had turned white, then slightly green, then run in the opposite direction down the corridor away from him. Okay, maybe it was more of a power walk than a run, but when Dominic told the story to Faith he expected to make it more of a sprint.

When he finally saw Faith, of course.

Maybe he'd pushed her too far last night, letting on that he knew she was lying to him. Faith was like a small frightened animal at times, behind her confident exterior. Whatever she was hiding, it scared her, which in turn worried Dominic even more.

Two and a half days. That was all the time he had left to uncover Faith's secret. To find out if it was something he could live with. Something they could deal with together.

And if it wasn't…then he had two and a half days before he never saw Faith again.

The thought made him shudder.

By the time he made it back to the hotel that evening, he had a scant half hour to shower and change, but he still managed to make it to the lobby before anyone else, ready for their evening of theatre.

Faith was next down, as he'd expected. He'd come to value the brief, quiet ten minutes before they left for the evening's entertainment. Ten minutes when it was just them and they had a chance to catch up on the day, and the plans for the next one. It was work, of course, but somehow it felt more like play when Faith was there.

The lift pinged, and Dominic turned to see if Faith was on board, sucking in a breath as the doors opened. Would it be backless? he wondered. And surely not black. Whatever it was, she'd look fantastic. And he'd get to spend the whole evening looking at her. Almost as good as if it were really just them going out together for the evening.

But then Faith stepped out of the lift, into the lobby, and Dominic's breath slowly released in disappointment.

'Sylvia let you buy that?' he asked as she strode across the lobby in plain flat navy shoes. What happened to the glorious red heels of last night? Oh yeah. Broken, even before she stamped on Jerry.

'What's wrong with it?' Faith asked, looking down at herself.

Dominic searched for the right words. In lots of ways, it was perfect. Navy dress, cream cardigan and handbag. Nothing too revealing or showy, but smart enough for the occasion. Maybe Sylvia *had* chosen it. He had a hard time believing Faith would because, despite everything that was right with it…

'It's just…boring.'

Faith beamed. 'Thank you. That's just what I was going for.'

Dominic shook his head. He was beginning to believe that he didn't stand a chance of ever understanding what went on in Faith's brain. Especially if he only had two days left to learn.

The others arrived shortly after, and they piled into pre-ordered taxis to take them to the theatre. There'd be food at the after-show party later, so he'd told Faith not to bother with booking a dinner.

The press were out in force for the occasion, and he lost sight of Faith in the melee as they were shepherded through the crowds into the theatre. Inside, the place was crowded with half familiar faces, and Dominic quickly lost track of who he actually knew and who he just recognised from TV.

'I've arranged drinks with the barman over in the balcony bar,' Faith said, suddenly at his side. She was shorter without her heels, and had to stand on tiptoe and shout into his ear to be heard over the crowd. Someone brushed past her and knocked her balance and, without even thinking about it, Dominic wrapped an arm around her waist to keep her upright.

'Lord Beresford?' Dominic looked up to see the official photographer for the evening brandishing a camera at him. 'A photo, if you please?'

He hated this. Hated that his attending a play was the cause for photographs and reports. Hated that anyone cared.

Still, it was part of the deal. He knew this. And, even if he hadn't, his father had made it perfectly clear when he was growing up. Whatever else was going on, you played the part.

One of the many things his father forgot after his mother left. Including his children.

He gave the photographer a swift nod and let his arm fall from Faith's waist.

'With your friend?' the photographer asked hopefully.

Of course. 'Do you mind?' he asked, turning to where Faith had been standing, only to find that she'd gone. He caught a brief glimpse of navy disappearing into the sea of people, but didn't bother calling after her. 'Apparently not,' he told the photographer, who looked disappointed, but snapped away at a couple of shots anyway.

He eventually found Faith, along with Sylvia and his clients, in the upper balcony bar. 'What happened to you?' he asked, taking a glass of champagne from her hand.

'Just doing my job,' she said, smiling innocently. 'Your guests were thirsty.'

She was lying again. He almost wished he couldn't tell. The number of casual lies she told him in a day was honestly disturbing.

'So, what's this show about, anyway?' he asked, to distract himself from the fact that not only was the woman he'd fallen for leaving him in two days, but she'd been lying to him the whole time he'd known her and it was getting increasingly likely that he'd never get to know the truth.

'You don't know?' she asked. 'But you specifically asked me to arrange for us to see it.'

He covered a yawn with his hand. Apparently late nights and long days weren't compatible with theatre visits. 'Sylvia said it was the biggest show opening this week. Although I think she just told me that so I'd get her a ticket, too.'

She stared at him. 'You're going to sleep through the whole thing, aren't you? The lights will go down, the theatre will be warm, the seats will be cosy, and I'll spend the entire evening trying to pretend you're not snoring.'

Actually, that didn't sound all that bad. 'I'm sure I'll wake up for the interval drinks.'

Faith rolled her eyes, but then he felt her body tense beside his.

'Lord Beresford? Perhaps I could get that shot of you with your friend now?'

Photographers. Knowing his luck, they'd get one of him fast asleep halfway through the first act. And now worrying about that was going to keep him awake.

'Faith? Is that okay?' He turned to where she'd been standing just moments ago, but the space was empty.

Where the hell had she gone now? And why?

'Sorry,' he told the photographer unapologetically. 'She's camera shy.'

And then he set about finding Faith, and some answers.

CHAPTER TEN

FAITH HAD FIGURED that the tiny alcove on the back stairs leading up to the Upper Circle was a decent enough place to hide. Plenty of people passing by, none of them likely to recognise a used-to-be-notorious girl in a boring navy dress.

She hadn't counted on Lord Dominic Beresford's tenacity, though.

'What the hell are you hiding from?' He planted himself outside her hiding place, hands on his hips.

'I'm not hiding,' Faith lied. 'I just got a bit claustrophobic. You know, with all the crowds up there. Thought I'd get some air.'

A group of theatre-goers trying to reach their seats forced Dominic off the staircase and into her alcove, and suddenly Faith really couldn't breathe. He was too solid, too attractive—and too close! How was she supposed to keep her story straight when she was surrounded by the scent of his aftershave, when she could feel the heat of his skin through his shirt?

'Claustrophobic.' Disbelief coloured Dominic's words. 'So you hid here. In a ridiculously small alcove with hundreds of people walking past.'

'I was *trying* to get outside,' Faith said, knowing he didn't believe her. 'I just got a little turned around.'

'Then let's go.' Grabbing her hand, Dominic led her down the staircase and out through a side door. Faith sucked in the cool evening air, letting it fill her lungs and calm her.

That had been close. Too close. If that photographer had got her photo and run it with a caption about Lord Beresford…it wouldn't matter where she went next, Dominic would still have to deal with the fallout when someone realised who she was.

He'd still end up hating her.

'Feeling any better?' Dominic asked as the side door slammed shut behind them.

Faith nodded. 'But I don't think we're getting back in that way,' she said, motioning at the handleless door. 'And I left our tickets in my bag, upstairs in the bar.'

'I'm fairly sure they'll let us back in.' Dominic leant back against the brick wall of the theatre, arms folded over his chest. 'If I ask them to.'

He was watching her too carefully and his words from the night before flooded her brain.

I just wish you'd stop lying to me and let me see the real you.

How did he know? And how much did he suspect?

'Are you going to?' she asked.

'That depends,' Dominic said.

'On what?'

'On if you're going to tell me the truth.'

Fear crawled through her middle. 'I told you. I just needed some air—'

'Not about tonight. Well, not just about tonight,' he amended. 'You've been lying to me since the moment we met, and I want to know why.'

Faith stilled, and looked up into his dark eyes.

'No,' she said. 'You really don't.'

* * *

Her words hit him in the gut. That was it then. Whatever her secret was, it was too big for them to move past. Too huge for her to even trust him with.

It was over, before it ever really started.

He should walk away now. Head back into the theatre and his clients and his sister. Let Faith work out the rest of the trip, without letting her any closer to his heart. Then he should put her on a plane and resign himself to never seeing her again.

He knew exactly what he should do.

But instead he said, 'Then we're not going back inside.'

She looked desperate now, her eyes wide and pleading. 'Dominic, don't be ridiculous. We've got your clients to sort out; my handbag is in there…'

'I'll text Sylvia. She can deal with everything.' In fact, he rather thought his sister might cheer approvingly.

'So what are we going to do?' Faith asked.

It wasn't a plan, wasn't something he'd thought out or weighed up and decided on. And it might be the most un-Lord-Beresford-like thing he'd done in his entire life.

But somehow Dominic knew it was the only thing to do.

'We're going to take a night off.'

'A night off?' Faith's forehead crinkled up.

He nodded. 'One night. Just one night, where I'm not Lord Beresford and you're not my employee. One night to just be Dominic and Faith.'

She wanted it, he could tell. Her eyes were wider than ever, filled with amazement, and the slight flush on her cheeks told him she hadn't missed any of the possibilities of the suggestion.

'For just this one night,' he said, moving closer, 'it doesn't matter about the truth. Doesn't matter about our pasts, or our futures. For tonight, all that matters is us.'

He took her hand, rubbing circles on her palm with his thumb, and held his breath when she looked up at him, her lower lip caught between her teeth.

'Just one night?'

'Just one night,' he echoed.

'What will we do?' she asked, and Dominic's mind filled with possibilities, most including getting her out of that ugly dress as soon as possible.

No. Too quick. If he only had one night with her, he needed to do this properly.

'First, I'm going to take you out for dinner. Anywhere you choose.'

Some of the tension dropped from her stance at that, and she smiled. 'I know just the place.'

The crowds were still gathered out front, but by keeping close to the side of the building they managed to avoid them as they dashed across the street behind the theatre, the warm evening air smelling of freedom and possibility.

One night. Just one night. That was what he'd said. And even though Faith knew she shouldn't, knew that this could end in disaster, or at least a broken heart, she couldn't resist that kind of temptation. Surely she could keep her secret for just one night?

Covent Garden buzzed with life, filled to overflowing with tourists, buskers, after-work socialisers, people wanting to sell something and people looking to buy. Faith let the sights and sounds warm her, make her feel at home again. She hadn't realised she'd felt so out of place in her own London that week, until now.

'So, where do you want to go?' Dominic asked. 'Somewhere around here?' He cast an arm around him at the market piazza, almost hitting a tourist in shorts and a Bermuda shirt as he did so. 'Looks like there's plenty of places to choose from.' Seeing Faith's horrified look, he added, 'What? I know it's not exactly up there with the meals you've been organising this week—'

'That's not it,' Faith interrupted. 'Just…Covent Garden's for the tourists. It's the equivalent of eating pizza right next door to the Coliseum in Rome. You'll get perfectly ordinary pizza at three times the price.'

They'd stopped walking, Faith realised, and were standing still in a sea of people, swelling and ebbing around them. Dominic's hand came down to rest at her waist, pulling her in closer, anchoring her against the tide. Heat spread out through her body from the place where they touched, and she swallowed, hard.

'Follow me,' she said, and grabbed his hand with her own.

It was easy to get trapped in the slow-moving crowds if you didn't know what you were doing. Dominic would have been far too polite to do the essential barging through if she'd left him to his own devices. That was the only reason she held his hand, she reasoned.

Of course, once they'd escaped the market and were walking more casually away along Long Acre, she didn't let go. By that point, it felt far too natural.

'Where are we going?' Dominic asked, his thumb rubbing the back of her hand in a relaxing rhythm.

'A little Italian I know.' Marco had taken her there, back when he was trying to hire her for his fledgling tour company. He said it would give her a real taste of Rome.

Dominic's thumb stopped its comforting movements. 'Missing Italy already?'

'Not really,' Faith said, giving him a smile. 'Mostly just the pasta.'

He returned the smile and started stroking her hand again.

Faith suddenly found herself wishing that she'd bought the dress Sylvia wanted her to have, the backless, wine-red dress that cascaded down her legs and showed off every single curve, instead of the boring navy shift she'd chosen.

Tugging on his hand, she led him down a hidden backstreet into the cooler shadows where the sun never reached, even at noon on midsummer. Halfway down the alley, a tattered red sign hung above a dirty window, and read simply, 'Lola's'. No one would recognise them there.

'This is it?' Dominic asked, looking dubious.

'Trust me,' Faith said, and he sighed.

'Seems to me, trusting you could get me into a lot of trouble.'

Faith smiled brightly to try and pretend that didn't hurt, just a little. After all, he was right. 'Oh, I don't know. You're doing okay so far.'

'This is true.' He pushed against the door and a bell clattered tinnily. 'Come on, then.'

Inside, the restaurant was even darker than Faith remembered. But then, most of her memories were of the picture Marco had painted of Rome in the summer, and of the Italian lakes. Well, that and the fantastic walnut pasta and red wine that went down like water.

A waiter in jeans and a T-shirt led them to a table at the back, and Faith watched in amusement as Dominic realised nearly every other table in the place was already occupied.

'Am I the only person who doesn't know about this place?' he murmured as they took their seats.

Faith slipped her cardigan from her shoulders and placed it on the back of her chair. White cashmere didn't go well with red wine. 'There are a lot of people in London,' she pointed out. 'Not everyone can afford to eat at the finest restaurants every night. Besides, the food's better here.'

'Can we see a menu, please?' Dominic asked, as if looking for proof, but the waiter shook his head.

'No menus,' he said, his rich Italian accent adding extra amusement to his tone. 'We'll bring you the best we have.'

As he spoke, a younger girl appeared, also in jeans, and filled their glasses with red wine. Dominic raised his eyebrows, but lifted the glass to his lips anyway.

'Not bad,' he said as the servers disappeared.

Faith tried her own. 'Liar. It's gorgeous.'

The smile Dominic gave her was warm and intimate, and suddenly Faith knew it didn't matter if the food had gone drastically downhill since the last time she was there; this would still be a better evening than the one with Marco. Apparently all she needed for a fantastic evening was the presence of Lord Dominic Beresford.

She wondered if that worked for everyone. She could use him on all her tours...

'What are you thinking?' Dominic asked, and Faith shook herself back into the real world. He wasn't Lord Beresford right now, anyway. He was just Dominic. Maybe even *her* Dominic, just for the night.

'Absolute nonsense,' she admitted. 'And worrying a little about abandoning my post.' Getting out of the theatre had seemed like the best plan, given that dodging every single camera was probably impossible. But, on the other hand, she'd been hired to do a job and she wasn't currently fulfilling those obligations.

'I'm the boss,' Dominic pointed out. 'You can look on this as…a mid-project appraisal.'

'Is that so?' Faith leant back in her chair and watched as he nodded. 'In that case, how am I doing?'

'Fantastically.'

Faith hoped the candlelight was forgiving enough to hide her blush. 'Anyone would think you were biased.'

Dominic's eyes turned dark. 'Oh, but I am.' Reaching across the table, he took her hand again. 'Utterly, utterly biased. Because I want you to stay in London with me.'

Maybe it was the wine, but suddenly Faith felt reckless. They weren't at the hotel, or at an event. There were no clients around. There was no chance of bumping into anyone who might recognise Lady Faith Fowlmere at Lola's. This was their one night. There was nothing at all to stop her asking for the truth.

'Because you want me to work for you?'

His smile was slow. 'Faith. I promise you that, for once, work is the furthest thing from my mind tonight.'

It wasn't quite a lie, Dominic reasoned and, even if it was, she'd told enough of her own. He'd offered her a night off, a night away from who they really were, because he couldn't bear the idea of her leaving without doing *something* about whatever compulsion it was that burned between them.

It wasn't easy, though. Business, sure. He could forget about contracts and meetings in a heartbeat. But the title, the heritage, they were scored deep into him in a way she couldn't understand. You had to be born to that kind of obligation. Still, just being with Faith made it easier. It was impossible not to relax around her, harder still not to lean into her, touch her, flirt and caress, however much he'd planned to take things slow.

Around the third glass of wine, he stopped even trying.

The servers, for all they looked as if they'd been yanked in off the streets, knew what they were doing. Dominic barely noticed when they topped up his glass or cleared away their empty plates. The food—incredible-tasting food on plates for sample-sized portions—just kept on coming, course after course. Antipasti, pastas—three kinds—fish, meat, and then, when they were almost fit to busting, a sorbet so sharp it almost cut the mouth. The tiramisu to finish would have been beyond him, but Faith grabbed her own spoon and dug into the shared plate, and the expression on her face as she tried it made him want to know what made her look like that. If he could replicate the experience for her in other ways...

'Oh, that is good,' he admitted, taking his own bite.

Faith gave him a smug smile. 'I knew you'd enjoy letting go for once.'

Suddenly, his head was filled with all the ways he could make her let go. How she would look if he kissed her breathless. How he could touch her until she forgot who she was, never mind him.

He swallowed down the last of his wine. Too much, too soon. 'So, what do you want to do next?' he asked, as the waiter brought over two tiny glasses of Limoncello, along with the bill.

Faith picked up her glass, took a sip, then licked her sticky fingers. Dominic felt something tighten in his chest at the sight. 'Well, that depends on you,' she said.

'On me? How?'

'Do you think you've managed to suitably forget who you are for the night?'

Watching her across the table in the candlelight, Dominic thought he might actually be a whole new person, after all. 'I think I've managed it, yes.'

'In that case,' she said, pushing his liquor glass towards him with two fingers, 'drink up. Because I want to show you *my* London.'

CHAPTER ELEVEN

She started on the South Bank, because she loved the way it lit up and came to life at night. They crossed at Waterloo Bridge, with a crush of other people heading the same way, and walked west along the river, towards the London Eye.

'I've been on that, at least,' Dominic said, looping her hand through his arm. 'Does that earn me any points?'

Faith considered. 'Depends. Did you go on an ordinary day with ordinary people? Or were there champagne, strawberries and schmoozing involved?'

'The latter,' Dominic admitted. 'Does that mean I have to go on it again?'

'Probably. But not tonight.'

They walked further, staring back across the river at the lights of Westminster, watching Big Ben as it chimed the hour. It was already getting late, Faith realised. She wondered how Dominic would feel about getting the night bus back... She shook her head. A step too far for this trip, she decided. Besides, if the evening went the way she hoped, she didn't want to waste time on buses.

'You know, I don't think I've ever done this,' Dominic said as they paused at the railings, just taking in the skyline.

'Done what?'

'Just…wandered around the city with a beautiful girl on my arm.' He tugged her a little closer at his words, and Faith felt the warmth of him seeping through her dress. He thought she was beautiful. No one had ever called her that before. Sexy, yes. Gorgeous, yes. Beautiful? No.

'How long have you lived here?' she asked, hoping to distract from her blush. 'How is that even possible?'

Dominic shrugged, and shifted again, drawing her into the circle of his arms, making her feel warm and safe. 'I grew up on the country estate. Trips to London were always for a purpose. I went from car to hotel to venue or event, back to hotel then car and home again. I wasn't exactly encouraged to explore.'

Faith leant back against his chest, remembering how that felt, that being shuffled from one place to the next, more of an accessory than a person. Surely Dominic, of all people, could understand why she'd run?

'What about when you grew up?' she asked.

'It didn't occur to me,' Dominic said, amused honesty in his voice. 'I don't know why. No, I do. There was just so much else to do. I had an entire family name to save. Every single thing I did, for years, was about building up the estate, making new connections, finding new ways to use the land, the influence, the money that started coming in. I didn't have time for anything else.'

'Not even people?' He sounded so lonely. How could she leave him when he sounded so terribly alone?

'Just Sylvia, really. Until Kat came along.'

Ah, of course. Maybe he had a reason for wanting to be alone. 'I don't like to pry…'

'You love to pry. You're officially nosy.'

'Okay, yes, I am.' How had he got to know her so well, so fast? 'I saw the YouTube video.'

'You and every other person in the country with eyes.' There was a bitterness to his words Faith didn't like. Was he still in love with Kat?

She tilted her head round to see his face. 'Want to tell me what happened?'

'You want a blow-by-blow account?' he asked, eyebrows raised. 'I thought you saw the video.'

'Not that,' she said. 'Between the two of you. A woman doesn't just go off and betray her fiancé on the Internet for no reason.'

He sighed, and she could feel the air leaving his chest, leaving him smaller, sunken. 'She didn't know she was being filmed, apparently. Not that it's much of an excuse.'

'It really, really isn't.'

There was a pause, and for a moment she thought that was all he would say on the matter. Then he spoke again. 'She was unhappy. With me, mostly. She…she wanted me to let her in, she said. She never felt like she was a real part of my life.'

Faith winced. She could see that, could see Dominic defending everything he held dear, holding it so tight that there was no room for anything else. Until tonight.

'You loved her, though?'

Dominic shrugged. 'She seemed like a good fit. Similar background, similar ambitions. She'd have been a great lady of the manor.'

Faith frowned. 'You make it sound like you were marrying her to enhance your brand, not because you loved her.'

'Maybe I was,' Dominic admitted, and Faith's eyes widened. 'Not intentionally, of course. I thought it was the real thing. But now, I wonder… Maybe she's right. Maybe I never let her in.'

'Because then she couldn't really leave you.'

She'd turned almost completely round in his arms now, Faith realised too late. His grip had tightened too, and anyone seeing them would surely have no doubt that they were lovers, held close in a lovers' embrace. Her body pressed up against his chest, her hands at his back. Would he kiss her this time? Would she let him?

Somewhere, a car horn blared, a crowd of guys laughed out loud and music played. Dominic ignored all of it, staring straight into her eyes. Then, without giving any indication of what had changed between them, he said, 'So, what's next on this tour of yours?'

Faith blinked, trying to break out of the moment. And then she realised that there was still one very special place she wanted to show him. 'Let's go see the pelicans.'

'Are you going to make me break into a zoo?' Dominic asked as they crossed back over Westminster Bridge, the Thames gleaming with lights below them. 'Because I think not being Lord Beresford for the night stops at criminal behaviour.'

Faith rolled her eyes, then tugged on his hand to make him keep moving. 'Have you honestly never seen the pelicans in St James's Park before?'

'Didn't even know we had any.' How many times had he walked through that park, on the way to somewhere? A few, at least. Wouldn't he have noticed big white birds swooping overhead?

The gates to the park were still open, thankfully, which meant it couldn't be too late, even if it felt like some magical witching hour. That was probably just Faith's influence.

'What time does the park close?' he asked as they headed into trees and lush grasses, just moments from the busy city centre.

'Midnight,' Faith replied, her tour guide brain still working.

'Do you know everything about London?' He'd lived in the city most of his adult life, and apparently missed everything of any importance. He had to spend more time exploring. If he ever got the chance.

'I know that the park has been home to pelicans since 1664, when the Russian Ambassador gave the first ones as a gift. And I know that the city of Prague gave the park three new ones last year, and I haven't met them yet.'

She talked about them like friends or relatives, he realised. 'You like the pelicans?'

'They're my favourite part of the city,' she admitted, stumbling to a stop on the lakeside path. 'Look!'

Dominic's gaze followed where her finger was pointing, into a clump of reeds at the edge of the lake. It took him a moment to spot the white feathers in the moonlight. 'It's asleep.'

Faith gave him a scathing look. 'Of course he is. It's late.'

Glancing at his watch, Dominic realised she was right. 'Eleven-thirty. Cars should be picking up from the theatre around now. Heading to the after-show party.'

'Want to head back and catch up with them?' Faith asked.

Dominic didn't even need to think about his answer. 'No.'

'So what do you want to do?' She was close again,

too close. Closer even than she'd been as they'd looked out over the river, talking about Kat. Close enough to make him crazy. 'It's your turn to choose.'

'I want to spend tonight with you.'

So close he could see her eyes darkening, even in the faint moonlight under the trees. 'I thought that's what we've been doing.'

He shook his head. 'This was just the evening. I want the whole night.'

And he did. He wanted it so badly he ached. And he didn't care if she couldn't stay, didn't care if it could never go anywhere. Didn't care what the risk was. He just wanted her.

'Are you sure?' Faith asked, her lower lip caught between her teeth.

'Absolutely.'

'I'm leaving—'

'I know. We both know what this is, and what it isn't. What it can't be. I don't know what you're hiding from me, but I trust you it's better that way. And I can't let you leave without...' He stopped, trying to find the words. Wrapping his hands around her waist, he pulled her closer, close enough that she had to be able to feel every line of his body through that hideous dress. 'You've shown me your world tonight. All the things you love about a city I've lived in for years and never got to see.' No, that wasn't right. 'Or, worse, all the things I've seen every day and never felt the way you do. I want one night to see everything through your eyes. Just one night.'

Rising up on tiptoe, Faith pressed her lips against his and his whole body almost sagged with relief. Then his brain caught up and he hauled her closer again, practically lifting her off the floor as he kissed her properly,

thoroughly. The way a woman like Faith deserved to
be kissed.

'Back to the hotel?' Faith asked when he finally
pulled away.

Dominic nodded. It was past time to take Faith home
to bed.

They caught a cab back to the hotel, Dominic's hand at
her waist the whole way, and Faith could feel the blood
thrumming through her veins too fast, driving her on.
He was Lord Beresford again now, she could tell, so
there was no inappropriate behaviour in the taxi, much
as she considered just climbing into his lap and kissing
him speechless.

Or maybe she'd be the one without words. But the
man could kiss! One touch of his lips and she'd forgotten anything she ever knew about any city in the world.
If someone had asked her where she was right then,
she'd have struggled to answer.

In a way, she was almost glad of the reprieve his
propriety gave her. She needed a moment to gather her
thoughts, to enjoy the anticipation of what was ahead.
And besides, with only one night to enjoy with him,
she wouldn't have wanted him to be pretending to be
anyone else.

No, against the odds, and despite everything, it was
Lord Dominic Beresford she'd fallen for, and Faith
didn't want to even pretend otherwise.

The taxi pulled up outside the hotel, and Dominic
handed over a couple of notes to the driver—too much,
probably, not that Faith cared right then. She glanced
around to check before getting out of the car, but there was
no sign of the service she'd arranged to collect the clients
from the theatre. She checked her phone quickly; no one

had called, so hopefully that meant they were all still having fun at the after-show party, somewhere they wouldn't see her and Dominic heading up to his suite together.

Perfect.

Dominic took her arm as they headed into the hotel, and she felt a certain relief that he wasn't hiding this. Wasn't hiding her. She'd worried he might be...embarrassed, if not ashamed. After all, as far as he was concerned she wasn't in his social strata and besides, she was his employee. Dominic wasn't the sort to blur the lines of propriety that way, even without the secrets he knew she was keeping.

The doorman at the hotel foyer gave no sign of anything out of the ordinary when they walked in. The concierge nodded politely, but otherwise kept a blank face. The receptionist barely even looked up. Faith held her breath. This might really happen. One night: one perfect night. She'd earned this much over the last few years of voluntary exile, surely? He never had to know who she was. What she'd done.

They were silent in the lift, a respectable few inches between them. She wondered if Dominic really felt so keenly about keeping up appearances and respectability that he wouldn't even touch her in an empty lift. Or was he just afraid, as she was, that if they touched again they wouldn't be able to stop...?

She got her answer the moment the door to the hotel suite swung shut behind them.

'Faith...' His hands were on her waist in a moment, pulling her closer into him, his lips descending before she could even think, even comprehend what they were doing here.

He reached for the zip at the back of her dress, tugging it down with impatient fingers, and Faith breathed with relief to be out of the stupid thing. What had she been thinking, trying to be anyone but herself around this man? He might not know her true name or identity, but he saw exactly who she was. He'd found her, under the disguise, and wanted her anyway.

Kisses ran across her neck, her shoulders, and she realised Dominic was whispering between each one, murmuring words of affection and longing and desire. She bit her lip, tilting her head to give him better access, and wondered if she'd ever stop being surprised by this man. This man who had looked at her body with distaste when they met, but was now admitting exactly how much he wanted it. This man who appeared every inch the respectable aristocrat every moment of the day, but was currently whispering exactly what he wanted to do to her in enough detail to make her whole body pulse.

He was so much more than she'd ever imagined that night in Rome, and she wanted him more than she could have dreamt.

Reaching up, she trailed her own kisses across his jaw, to his ear, his hands gripping her tighter as she went. Then she whispered, 'Take me to bed,' and felt the floor disappear under her feet as he lifted her and turned them round, covering the space between them and the bed in a very few steps.

Faith's back hit the mattress and her greedy hands pulled him down on top of her, not wanting their bodies to be separated for a moment. This was it. Her one night with Dominic Beresford. One night to be entirely herself, whatever name she used. And she was definitely going to make the most of it.

Afterwards, in the dim light of the darkened room, Faith curled closer into Dominic's side and tried to control her breathing. 'We definitely have to do that again,' she said without thinking, then winced. 'Before I leave, I mean.'

'We really, really do,' Dominic said, and she relaxed. But then he added, 'You have to leave?'

She nodded against his chest, pressing a kiss against his breastbone as an apology. 'I do.'

'Why?'

It was easier, admitting things in the dark. 'I can't be who I need to be, here.'

'With me?'

'In London,' she corrected him.

He sighed. 'And I can't leave. Not for ever, anyway.'

If he were anyone else, he could, Faith knew. Anyone but Lord Dominic Beresford, defender of reputation and honour across the British Isles.

'The estate.'

'My family.'

'Your name.' She hadn't meant it to sound bitter, but it did.

Dominic shifted, turning onto his side and pulling her closer against him. She could only just see his eyes in the darkness, but she could feel his heartbeat against hers. 'It's not just the name. It's who I am. Who I was born to be.'

'You were someone else tonight,' she reminded him.

'Just for tonight. I wish…' He shook his head. 'I know you don't get it, Faith. And maybe it is just the way I was brought up, or my heritage. But…these things matter to me. Responsibility. Trust. Duty. Reputation. They do, and I can't change that. My mother…she didn't take those things seriously. She put her own desires ahead of her responsibilities and it almost destroyed us. She betrayed all of us when she ran away, but the family name most of all. I couldn't do that. And then Kat…'

Faith's heart grew heavy at the other woman's name. 'She betrayed your trust.'

'She did. But more than that... It wasn't just that she cheated on me. It was that she did it in a way calculated to cause the most damage to everything I hold dear. My family, my reputation. She hurt them. And she hurt me.'

He spoke simply, stating the facts, but the iron weight that had settled in Faith's chest in place of her heart pulled her down further at his words. Wasn't she doing the same? Whichever way things went. She was a runaway, a betrayer just like his mother. And she was making him take a risk of scandal and embarrassment, without even letting him know the danger was there, just like Kat. She should have told him, and now it was too late.

But if she'd told him...they'd never have had this night. And Faith couldn't give that up, even for honour's sake. Maybe that was the true difference between them.

A sharp ringing noise jerked her out of her thoughts, and Dominic reached across her body to grab the hotel room phone.

'Yes?' he said, then as he listened to the voice on the line his body stilled. 'We'll be right down.'

Hanging up, he pulled away from Faith, sitting with his back to her on the edge of the bed.

'What's happened?' she asked, her heavy heart beating too hard now.

Dominic's voice was calm and steady as he replied. Unfeeling. 'They need us in the lobby. There's someone down there asking for you. Apparently he's causing quite a scene.'

Oh no. Faith swallowed, reaching for her dress. 'Right, of course. I don't...I can't...' How could she explain that she didn't know who it was, because there

were too many options to choose from? Her father. Antonio. Great-Uncle Nigel. Who'd found her? And who
had such awfully bad timing as to ruin this night?

'I suppose we'll find out what this is about when we
get downstairs,' Dominic said, and Faith nodded, a sick
feeling rising up in her throat.

She didn't bother with her bra or tights, just pulled
the dress over her head and shoved her feet into her
shoes. She probably looked a state but, well, wasn't that
just what people would expect anyway? Even Dominic,
in trousers and an untucked shirt, looked less respectable than normal. Not as free and abandoned as he'd
been half an hour before, but Faith knew, in her heart,
that she'd never get to see that side of Dominic again.
Whoever was waiting for her in the lobby had ruined
that for her.

The lift ride down was silent again, but this time the
tension between them was filled with questions rather
than anticipation. Faith kept her eyes on the toes of her
shoes and prayed that she'd be able to talk her way out
of whatever this was.

But then the lift door opened and before they could
even step out she heard her name being yelled across
the lobby.

'Faith!'

She froze. The accent was wrong for Antonio, or her
father, and Great-Uncle Nigel sounded like the fifty-a-
day smoker he was, so…

'Lady Faith Fowlmere.'

Dominic froze beside her, and Faith made herself
look across the lobby to see who it was that had un-
masked her. Who had ruined her one night.

She closed her eyes against the horror as she recognised the photographer from the theatre striding across

the lobby towards her. Then her brain processed what she was seeing and her eyelids flew open again. He had his camera. He had his camera out and pointed at them.

'We need to go,' Dominic said, grabbing her hand, but Faith knew it was already too late. The flash of the camera lit up the subdued lobby, light reflecting off the marble tiles and the mirrors on the stairs. There was no hiding this now.

'You need to come with me. Now!' Dominic's words fought their way out from between clenched teeth and Faith ducked her head, turning and following him towards the lift.

'Lady Faith! Would you like to make a comment on your whereabouts for the last couple of years?' the photographer called after them, still snapping away.

'Do not say a single word.' He sounded furious. She'd known he would be. She'd just hoped he'd never have to find out. Or at least that she'd be many, many miles away when he did.

'Or perhaps what made you want to come back?'

Faith couldn't resist a glance over her shoulder at that, even as Dominic stabbed the call lift button repeatedly. The reporter was smirking, obviously assuming he knew exactly why she was there: Dominic. Just as they'd been so, so sure they knew what she was doing in that hotel room with Jared three years ago.

They were wrong again.

She hadn't come back to London for Dominic, and there wasn't a chance in hell he'd let her stay now he knew the truth.

The lift pinged and the doors opened at last. Dominic hauled her inside, holding down the close doors button before she was even through. All Faith could see was the reporter's smile, even after the lift started to move.

And then she realised she was alone with Dominic. Again.

'My room,' he said, the words clipped. 'We don't talk about this until we are safely behind a locked door.'

CHAPTER TWELVE

THIS WASN'T QUITE how he'd imagined having her in his room tonight.

Faith stood against the wall by the bathroom, arms folded over her chest, looking like a schoolgirl caught smoking. Like she was just anyone. Like she was still his Faith, only guiltier.

Lady Faith Fowlmere. How had he not known? Okay, so he didn't exactly study the social pages, but even he'd heard the story of the missing heiress, and the scandals she left behind. There must have been a clue, something that he'd missed. Probably because he was too busy being swayed by her curves and her enthusiasm for life.

A life away from the one he lived.

'Were you planning on telling me?' he asked, his eyes landing on her bra, still tossed across the arm of the chair. Just how had this gone so wrong so quickly?

Faith's head jerked up and she met his gaze head-on, her eyes wide but steady. 'No.'

Hope drained out of him. If she'd said anything else—that she was scared, that she hadn't known how, that she wanted to know how he felt first…anything else at all—maybe they could have worked it out. He could have understood, perhaps.

But she'd never wanted him to know who she was. Ever.

'Why?'

A half-shrug, one hunched shoulder raised. 'We agreed one night. Come on. You knew I wasn't going to stay, and you knew there was a reason. Look me up on the Internet and you'll see why. I'm a scandal; everyone knows it. And I know you. You'd have fired me if you found out. Too much of a risk. And, more than that, you'd have wanted me to talk to my parents, to reconcile, for the good of the family name. You know you would.'

She was right. She did know him. Better than he'd ever been allowed to know her. 'And you won't.' Not a question. He knew her that well, at least.

'I don't ever want to go back there.' The vehemence in her voice surprised him. He didn't know the Fowlmeres personally, but they were her family.

'You might have to. We need to put a respectable face on this, and "runaway heiress returns home" sounds a hell of a lot better than "runaway heiress found in high-priced love nest".' He reached for his phone, trying to keep his temper under control. He needed to think, not react. And he needed to ignore the part of his brain that was telling him that the secrets were out now. He knew the worst of it. Maybe he could salvage something from this.

But first he had to fix it.

'Here's what's going to happen now,' he said, scrolling through his contacts. 'I'm going to call my PR people, get them down here. I'll sit down with them, come up with a plan. Maybe we can talk to the reporter, or more likely the newspaper owner. Maybe we can get an injunction. I don't know. But I am *not* going to let your past ruin my future.'

Faith hadn't even moved from her position by the door. 'And what am I going to be doing, while you set about fixing my mistakes?' Her voice was cool, calm—everything he didn't feel right then.

'You are going to be sitting in your hotel room, not talking to anyone, not seeing anyone, not even *thinking* about anyone. Do you understand me?'

Her eyes were sad as she spoke. 'Oh, I understand. You're going to rewrite not just my history, but our entire past.'

'I've known you a week, Faith. I don't think what we had qualifies as a past.'

'We had tonight.'

'And now we don't.'

Faith felt very cold, as if someone had left a window open in winter and the icy wind was chilling her through, layer by layer. Was this how it felt to freeze to death? And, in the absence of both winter and wind, was Dominic's coldness enough to finish the job?

'You're treating me like a child,' she said, the words hard lumps in her throat.

'I'm treating you like what you are,' he replied. 'A scandal and a flight risk.'

Just like his mother, Faith realised. But knowing why he was mad, expecting it even, didn't make it any easier.

And it didn't mean he got to take over her life.

'I understand,' she said again, wrapping her arms tighter around her. 'You'd better make your phone call.'

Dominic gave a sharp nod. 'Go straight to your room. I wouldn't put it past that photographer to have snuck back in, assuming security kicked him out by now. He could be anywhere. I'll call you in the morning,' he said, and she nodded as she collected her belongings and headed back towards the door, away from him, thinking hard.

He wanted her to stay hidden. Wanted her to let him fix her life for her. Wanted her to be a good, obedient Lady Faith.

It was as if he'd never known her at all.

This would be all over the Internet by the morning, however hot Dominic's PR team were supposed to be. And if she were going to be a story again, a scandal even, she was doing it on her own terms. She couldn't stay with someone who was embarrassed by her, ashamed of her.

Not even Dominic.

The story was out now, and that changed everything. What was the point of hiding when everyone knew where she was? This job had been her last chance. Without it—and without her salary for the week—she was out of options. She couldn't just hop on a flight to another country this time. Chances were, she'd be spotted at the airport, anyway.

No, Faith knew what she needed to do next. Even if it was the last thing she wanted.

Back in her hotel room, Faith packed quickly and economically. Three years as a tour guide had taught her the best way to roll clothes, as well as what was essential, and what wasn't.

She stripped off the hideous dress she'd bought for the theatre and left it folded on the chair. She wouldn't need it again. Instead, she pulled on an old pair of jeans, a T-shirt and a cardigan, loading her case with the rest of her clothes. She removed her make-up before packing her cosmetics bag, shoved her feet in her trainers and headed for the door.

As one final thought, she left Dominic's expenses credit card on top of the dress. He already thought badly enough of her. She didn't want him thinking she was a thief, too.

She kept the money in her purse though, the last remains of the petty cash he'd given her at the start of the week, to buy a train ticket back to the only place she had left.

Home.

Dominic was up early the next day, after a night spent liaising with his PR team and barely sleeping. He could still smell Faith on the bed sheets, and knowing she was only a few rooms away, awaiting his decision on her future, didn't help. He knew he couldn't really have handled it differently, under the circumstances. But knowing that didn't make him feel any better about it.

Now he just had to break the plan to Faith.

'We'll sell it as a rehabilitation,' Matthew the PR guy had said once they'd established there was no way to keep the news that the runaway heiress was back in town from breaking. 'You met in Rome and brought her back to try and reconcile her with her parents. There'll still be a lot of talk about her past, I'm sure, but as long as we present it right, get in early with the story, you should both come out okay.'

The first step, they'd agreed, was to get Faith to give an interview, with Dominic at her side as a sort of mentor. Then they'd stage the reunion with her parents, build it up carefully. After that, Matthew said, Dominic could wash his hands of her altogether, if he wanted.

It was a plan. It wasn't perfect, but it should at least

minimise the damage. Once he convinced Faith to play along.

Showered and dressed, he headed to her room, annoyed when she didn't answer his knock. He banged louder, and this time the door opened—only there was nobody on the other side. Anger and frustration started to build. The room was empty, with no sign that anyone had even slept in the bed last night.

Dominic swore. The runaway heiress had run again.

'I'm not staying,' Faith said, the moment her mother opened the door. Time was, there'd have been the butler to do that, but after Jenkins died when Faith was seven, there'd never been the money to hire another one.

Her mother raised her eyebrows at her, gestured inside with her glass and said, 'Then I assume you want money. There isn't any, you know.'

'Trust me,' Faith said, lugging her suitcase over the threshold, 'I know.'

Her father, at least, seemed pleased to see her.

'We missed you around here, you know,' he said, kissing her cheek and taking her arm as if she'd been away on holiday, not missing for three years. 'Nobody to laugh at my jokes!'

'I can't imagine that's true.' There had always been someone to laugh at the right time, to sparkle and smile when he wanted it. Lord Fowlmere had never needed his daughter—or even his wife—for that.

He laughed. 'Dahlia! Fix this girl a cocktail. She's probably been travelling for days to return to the bosom of her family.'

In fact, Faith had caught the first train north from King's Cross, studiously avoiding all the papers at the station and refusing to log into the train Wi-Fi. Instead, she'd slept all the way, then walked the three miles from the nearest station and arrived at Fowlmere late morning. Also known as cocktail hour to her mother and father.

While her mother fixed her drink, Faith took herself and her suitcase back up to her old room.

Now she was back, it almost felt as if she'd never left, except for the aching loss in her middle where thoughts of Dominic used to reside. If she thought about him, about the disappointment on his face or the feel of his body against hers, she'd cry. And if she started, she might not stop. So, no crying.

But, seriously, why was it she cared so much about his disappointment? She'd let down every single member of her family, scandalised the society in which they lived…why would she care about disappointing one man who she'd known for less than a week? Especially one who'd wanted her to stay put and stay quiet while he managed her life.

The answer whispered around her mind, but Faith refused to acknowledge it. That way lay madness, and probably a lot more cocktails than was advisable.

She managed to avoid most of her parents' questions by hiding in her room until dinner, ostensibly napping. Her father blamed jet lag and let her be, which was a blessing. But Faith knew she'd never sleep until she faced things head-on. So she pulled out her tablet, took a deep breath and checked out the damage.

The blogs and the websites had the news first, as always. The photo of her and Dominic in the lobby of the Greyfriars, looking as if they'd just rolled out of bed, was plastered everywhere. Faith scrolled past, wishing that every glimpse of the picture didn't make her remember exactly what they had been doing just before it was taken. How his body had felt pressed against hers. How perfect everything had been, for one fleeting moment.

The text below tended to be scant. Nobody knew anything except that she had been seen in London with Lord Dominic Beresford. Which was, she supposed, all there really was to know—especially if Dominic's PR team had got to work. There was speculation about where she'd been, and whether she was still holed up at the Greyfriars, but that was it for new news.

So, of course, they rehashed the old news instead. Faith buried the tablet under a pile of blankets on the trunk at the end of the bed when she reached that part.

Dinner with her parents was a stilted affair. Dad would try to make jokes, telling anecdotes that grew more obscure and confused with every glass of wine, but neither her mum nor Faith laughed. When he pulled out the whisky after dinner, Faith thought of Dominic and declined.

'I need an early night,' she said.

Her mother frowned. 'You slept all afternoon.'

'Jet lag, Dahlia,' Dad said, and Faith didn't disagree.

She wandered through the halls of the manor towards the main staircase, her gaze alighting on the holes in the carpet, the empty spaces on the shelves where expensive trinkets once sat. In some ways, it was hard not to compare Fowlmere with Beresford Hall. In others... there just was no comparison.

Fowlmere was decaying, ruined. Over. Just like her relationship with Dominic.

Tucked up in her childhood bed, the old feelings of isolation and hopelessness pressed in on her, but she willed them away. She'd escaped from this place once. She'd do it again. This was merely a temporary stop, until everything blew over and she was employable again. That was all.

She would never have to be that Lady Faith again. The girl with no place in the world, whose very home was falling apart around her, whose parents couldn't see past their own problems to see her misery. She was an adult now, and she got to choose her own life.

And nobody in their right mind would choose this.

The next morning, Faith pulled her tablet out from its cocoon and braved the news sites again. Nothing much new, except a note that Dominic had checked out of the Greyfriars, but with no sign of her. There was a new photo, showing Dominic stalking out of the hotel, dark eyes hard, ignoring every single reporter and photographer waiting for him. Something pulled at Faith's insides at the sight of him.

How he must hate her right now.

She shook her head. She had more practical matters to worry about. The news would have made it from the Internet to the papers this morning, which meant that her father would read it. And if the world knew she was no longer at the Greyfriars, the paparazzi would be coming here next. She needed to warn her parents, see if they were willing to stick with a 'no comment' rule until the reporters got bored. After all, none of them were very likely to want to sit in a field outside a crumbling mansion for more than a day or two, even if it meant getting a photo of the Runaway Heiress.

But before she got further than pulling on her dressing gown against the pervasive chill of Fowlmere Manor there was a sharp rap on the door and a mug of tea poked into the room, followed by her father.

'Am I allowed in?'

'Of course.' Faith took the drink and sipped. Milk and two sugars. She hadn't taken sugar for years.

Entering, he moved to the bed and sat, bouncing a little on the mattress. 'I haven't been in here for a while,' he admitted. 'Your mother, she'd come and sit in here whenever she missed you, but I found it easier just to stay away. Much like yourself.'

Faith blinked. 'She missed me?'

'Oh, very much. We both did. Not just for the laughing at jokes thing.' He gave her his trademark lopsided smile. 'And then when I saw that business in the papers this morning...I understood. No jet lag then, I suppose?' A blush heated Faith's cheeks. 'Shame you couldn't bring Lord Beresford with you, really. I wouldn't mind picking his brain on a few subjects.'

'It's not...we're not...' Faith swallowed. 'It wasn't how I imagine they made it look. Not really. And anyway, it didn't end well.'

'But it is ended?' her father asked. 'That's a pity. He's done incredibly well, really, given what he started with.'

Faith rather thought that Dominic had done incredibly well for anyone, but that wasn't her main concern. She could see her father calculating what he could do with access to a fortune like the Beresfords'. How there might be the chance of a little loan, something between friends. She'd seen it before. But not again.

'No. It's definitely over,' she said.

'Ah, well.' He shifted on the bed, kicking up his feet. 'Your mother tells me you're not planning on staying.'

'That's right.' Faith sat down on the dressing table stool and took a sip of her too sweet tea. 'I've just finished a job down in London. I should be able to pick up another one fairly quickly.' As long as they didn't want references from Dominic. Or Marco... 'Once I'm sorted, I'll move out again. But I might be able to send some money home, to help out.' It would just go onto the gin budget, she knew, but at least she might feel a little less guilty.

'What sort of a job?' her father asked, curiosity in his gaze. When she gave him a look, he threw up his hands to protest his innocence. 'It's not like we have any idea what you've been doing for the last few years. Or even where you've been, except for the news that you apparently somehow fell in with Beresford.'

Guilt pinged at her middle again. Okay, so they'd been lousy parents for the most part, and it hadn't really occurred to her that they might be worried about her whereabouts, but she could have at least dropped them a postcard, or something.

Except they'd have dragged her back. Although, right now, she wasn't sure if that might not have been a good thing. She'd never have met Dominic. Never ended up in this hideous mess.

But she could never really wish not to have met Dominic.

'I've been working as a tour guide,' she said, reaching for her mug again. 'In London, and in Italy.'

'A tour guide?' Her father looked fascinated. The idea of work had always been interesting to him. Just a shame he'd never had the desire to actually do any himself. 'Showing people around things?'

'And organising their hotels, their travel, looking after their needs, their trips and so forth. Yes.'

'Sounds like being a servant,' her father said, and laughed. 'Did you have to wear a uniform?'

Faith nodded. Who was he to suggest that her job was below her station? At least she was doing more than sitting around drinking in a decaying relic of an earlier era. 'I did. And actually it was fun. I liked it, and I'm good at it. So I'll find another job doing the same sort of thing, uniform and all if required, and send some money home for the drinks cabinet. Okay?'

'Whatever makes you happy, buttercup,' he said, instantly making her feel bad for acting so defensive. It really was just like old times. 'Only I was just thinking that it might be you don't have to go all that far to find that new job of yours.'

Faith felt her parental sixth sense tingle. This wasn't going to be good. 'I was thinking London...close enough to visit, right?' Not that she intended to. But if she could borrow the car to get to the station, she could commute from Fowlmere until she had enough cash to find a place of her own.

Her father shook his head. 'I've got a better idea. You want to be a tour guide? You can do that right here. At Fowlmere!'

Faith thought of the entrance hall, with its dingy lighting and faded and fraying curtains in the windows. So different to the bright open halls and lovingly restored features at Beresford Hall. 'Dad, I really don't think anyone is going to want to tour Fowlmere at the moment.' The whole house was in the same state. Who paid money to see mould and decay?

'Not yet, maybe, but I've got a plan.' He tapped the side of his nose.

Faith bit her lip to hold in a sigh. Just what she needed. Another one of Dad's plans.

'Perhaps, in the meantime, it might be better if I—'

'You want to go to London; I understand that.' Dad waved a hand around. 'That's fine. I need you in London. You can come to my meetings with me.'

'Meetings?' Dad's meetings only usually took place

in the pub, with men who knew exactly which horse was going to come in, really this time, honest.

He nodded. 'I've met with a young guy who is helping me save this place—for a cut, of course. Still, it might fill the old coffers again.'

Because that was what it was all about for her dad, wasn't it? Living the life he truly believed he was entitled to, even if they couldn't afford it. 'What does he intend to do?' she asked, as neutrally as she could manage.

'Do this place up. Use the land for corporate activities, events, the whole deal. Like Beresford did down at his place. I'll introduce you tomorrow; he can tell you all about it.'

The image of Beresford Hall, all clean and crisp facilities, clashed horribly with Fowlmere in Faith's memory. 'I think it might take a bit more work than you're anticipating, Dad. I've been to Beresford Hall. It's pretty spectacular.'

Her father smiled a beatific smile. 'That's why it's so wonderful that you're home to help me. Serendipity, don't you think?'

Fate was playing with her, just like it had at that airport bar in Rome. Her father looked so excited, so full of self-belief. But all Faith could feel was her escape routes closing in on her with every word.

CHAPTER THIRTEEN

THREE WEEKS LATER and still the world didn't seem ready to let him forget about Faith and move on.

The first week had been the worst. Once the picture of Dominic and Faith looking dishevelled together at the Greyfriars hit the Internet it was in every single paper by the evening editions. And then came worse—the photographer who'd caught them leaving the theatre hand in hand. Footage of Westminster Bridge that evening where someone's camera phone just happened to catch them embracing in the back of a photo. An anonymous source—Dominic suspected Jerry—who detailed how long Faith had worked for him and claimed 'they always seemed like they had some big secret. Like they were laughing at us behind our backs.'

There were more stories after that. Someone—presumably a friend Faith had spoken to when setting up the events that week—told the story of Faith talking her way into the job over drinks at the airport. It read as far more sordid than Dominic remembered the reality being, and even Sylvia had called him up and squealed at him, demanding to know if that was really what had happened.

And then Faith's apparently numerous ex-boyfriends

had started getting in on the act, and Dominic had stopped reading the stories.

But he couldn't avoid the headlines. Ridiculous puns and alliterations that no one showed any sign of getting bored with. 'Runaway Heiress, Runaway Bride?' was the latest one. Dominic hadn't quite managed to restrain himself from reading the entire speculative article that followed that one, suggesting that Faith had left him just after he'd proposed marriage.

The worst of it was, with every article he learned something new about Faith—although he'd probably never know for sure what was truth and what was pure fabrication.

He'd learned about her family, finally making sense of the bits and pieces she'd told him. No wonder she'd hated being at Beresford Hall. By all accounts, her father had spent his way through the Fowlmere fortune in record time. He must have been a constant reminder of what she'd lost.

He'd followed the story of her misspent youth, too. The media had happily mined the photo archive with every article, although Dominic had barely recognised his Faith in the scantily clad, drunken society girl falling out of nightclubs and being caught on camera with the hot young celebs of the day.

His Faith. That was one thing she'd never been, not really.

In fact, if the papers had it right, if she was anyone's Faith it was Jared Hawkes's, the married rock star with a notorious drug problem who had, apparently, left his wife and kids for Faith, before she skipped the country.

She looked more like he remembered her in the photos of her leaving the hotel with Hawkes, which somehow made things worse.

He'd tried to keep his head down and focus on work, wait for it all to blow over like Matthew the PR guy advised. But even if Sylvia was reporting record numbers of visitors to Beresford Hall, the Americans had returned home leaving the contracts unsigned, after many awkward conversations and superior looks from Jerry. So now he was waiting. Waiting to see if his professional life could move past this scandal. Waiting to see when the next comparison piece between his mother and Faith would appear in the papers. Waiting, against reason, for Faith to suddenly appear in his life again, the way she had the first time.

Because, the truth was, London wasn't the same without Faith. She'd already been gone longer than she'd been with him, but in three weeks that feeling of something being missing hadn't faded. In the office, he missed her snarky emails pinging through every so often. In his apartment, he missed the idea of her sprawled across his sofa, tablet on her lap, sipping whisky. And in the city...well, that was the worst.

It seemed that everywhere he went there were reminders of her. A poster for a show she'd wanted to see. A view of Tower Bridge and the memory of the dress she'd worn to dinner that night. A tiny backstreet Italian restaurant that was never Lola's, but often looked close. A pelican staring balefully at him in St James's Park.

He seemed to be, inexplicably, spending a lot of time walking through St James's Park these days. He couldn't even remember how he used to get from one place to another, before Faith introduced him to the pelicans.

The most embarrassing part was that he kept thinking he saw her. All across London, any time he spotted a woman in a red cardigan, or wild dark hair, his brain screamed 'Faith!' Several times, he'd found himself halfway to accosting a curvy stranger before he realised that, even if it was her, she'd betrayed him, she'd run away from him, and they were done.

He had a list of things he wanted to say to her, though. A mental list he added to each night when he couldn't sleep, remembering the feel of her body against his, under his.

It started with the obvious. *Why couldn't you just do as I asked you for once?* If she'd just stayed, he could have fixed things. She knew that, surely? How desperate must she have been to get away from him that she ran anyway?

Just one night. That had been the agreement. Which led to the second item on his list. *Why didn't you want to stay?*

Except that sounded too desperate, as if there were a hole in his life waiting for her to fill it, even after all that she'd done, so he always mentally scratched that one off again.

The list went on and on, through anger, pain, loss and outright fury. But the last question was always the same. *Why couldn't you have just left me alone in that airport bar?*

Because if he'd never met Faith, his life wouldn't be so disordered, so confused. And people wouldn't be discussing his private life again, the way they had after the revelations about his mother's affair.

And that, he had to admit, was the part that made him angriest of all.

But the dark-haired woman across the street, or the park, or the shop was never Faith, so he never got to ask her any of the things on his list.

No one seemed to know where she was, but Dominic assumed she'd skipped abroad again. The reporters had staked out Fowlmere for a few days after he checked out of the Greyfriars and it became clear she was no longer there with him. He'd read a brief statement from Lord Fowlmere saying that his daughter was just fine, thank you, but taking a little time off. No hint on where she might be doing that. Dominic couldn't even be sure that the man really did know where Faith was.

The search for the runaway heiress had reached a dead end.

Until, unexpectedly, one evening, at a charity ball Sylvia had insisted he attend, the woman across the room really was Faith, and he didn't even recognise her.

'Look!' Sylvia nudged him in the ribs, hard, just in case he'd missed her not-at-all-discreet attempt at a stage whisper.

Dominic straightened his dinner jacket. 'Where, exactly, am I looking?'

'Over there! Cream dress. Gorgeous skin. Hair pinned back.'

He followed her also-not-discreet pointing finger with his gaze. 'Still not getting it,' he said. Except he was. There was something. Not in the polite expression of interest on the woman's face as she listened to some bore drone on. And not in the high-cut evening dress, complete with pearls. But underneath all that...

'It's Faith, you idiot!' Sylvia prodded him in the ribs again. 'You need to go and talk to her.'

Around him, the room was already starting to buzz. Whispers of his name and hers. Those looks he thought he'd left behind years ago, the ones that said: *We know your secrets.*

What was she doing here? Shouldn't she be in Italy or Australia or anywhere by now? Not standing next to her father at the most glamorous, most publicised and photographed charity ball of the year.

Had she really gone home? The journalists must have grown bored of staking out a crumbling estate in the middle of nowhere pretty quickly not to have noticed. But if her big plan was to go home anyway, why couldn't she have just stayed long enough for him to fix things?

He had to leave. He'd drop a large enough donation to the charity to excuse his absence at the ball, and he'd be gone. No way he was providing entertainment to a room full of gossip hounds by actually talking to Faith.

'People are starting to stare,' Sylvia pointed out, as if he hadn't noticed.

'Let them.' Dominic slammed his champagne flute onto a passing waiter's tray. 'I'm leaving.'

'Dominic, no.' Sylvia grabbed the sleeve of his jacket and held on, her brightly polished nails digging into his arm through the fabric. 'Look, the only way this blows over is if you and Faith act like it doesn't matter. You can't be all affronted and embarrassed. You have to bore them out of it.'

'I'm not talking to her.' Just looking at her, acting the perfect heiress she'd never been before, had made it perfectly clear she couldn't be for him… It made his teeth ache his jaw was clenched so hard.

'Well, if you won't, I will,' Sylvia said, marching off across the room before Dominic could react.

Any eyes that weren't on him before swivelled round to catch the scene.

Bore them, she'd said. Somehow, Dominic suspected that wasn't the most likely outcome of this situation.

'Of course, I've always found…' Lord Hassleton said, and Faith tuned out again, secure in the knowledge that the peer liked the sound of his own voice far too much to ever expect her to comment on what he was actually saying. As long as she nodded occasionally and kept a polite smile on her lips, she'd be fine. And maybe one day, if she was really lucky, one of those waiters with the trays of champagne would come her way and give her another glass. Or brain Lord Hassleton with the silver tray. She wasn't fussy.

This was her role, for now. She'd got her parents to keep quiet about her return, hiding out in her room until the photographers outside Fowlmere Manor grew bored. But it seemed her father was deadly serious about them working together on the regeneration. She couldn't hide for ever, not if they were going to save the Manor, he said. They needed to get out there, meet people, start making new connections, new networks. And no one pulled a guilt trip quite like her father, so here she was, shaking hands, smiling politely and wishing she was anywhere else in the world.

It was only until her father got everything up and running, she told herself. After the intense interest about her return in the media, she needed this new boring Faith to make people forget her past. Then she could get on with fixing her future.

'Faith!' The bright voice to her left made Faith freeze. She didn't relax one iota when she realised who it was.

'Oh, Lord Hassleton,' Sylvia said, her tone light and happy and lots of other things Faith wouldn't really expect from Dominic's sister. 'I'm *so* sorry to interrupt. But you don't mind if I steal Lady Faith away from you for just a moment or two, do you? It's been an *age* since I saw her, and I'm *dying* to catch up.'

Lord Hassleton looked down at Sylvia's petite hand on his chubby arm and said, 'No, no, of course not. You gels go and…talk, or whatever.' He turned to Faith, and she quickly twisted her lips back into the fake smile she'd perfected in the mirror. 'We'll continue this another time, Lady Faith.'

'I look forward to it,' Faith lied.

But as she turned away from Lord Hassleton and let Sylvia lead her across the room, she started to think she might have had a better time listening to another hour's rambling on sewage works near his estate, or whatever it was the man had been going on about.

Just steps away stood Dominic, watching her with wary eyes. How had she not noticed him come in? Too busy trying to stay awake while listening to Lord Hassleton drone on, she supposed. But now… Now she could feel the stares on her back, the anticipation in the room. Everyone knew they'd been together. Everyone knew she hadn't been seen again since, until tonight. And everyone was waiting to see what would happen next.

'I don't think this is a good idea, Sylvia,' she said, slowing to a halt.

'Trust me, it is.' Sylvia tucked a hand through Faith's arm and dragged her forward, smiling like a politician. 'Like I told him, the only way this ends is if you two act like it doesn't matter.'

But it does matter, Faith didn't say.

'Faith,' Dominic said as they reached him, his voice cold and clipped. 'I wouldn't have expected to see you here.'

'I lost a bet,' Faith joked, and watched as Dominic's eyebrows sank into a frown.

Sylvia glanced between them, eyes wide. 'You know what? I think maybe I'd better leave you two to this.'

'Probably safest,' Faith agreed with a nod. Then,

glancing around the room, she watched as every person there suddenly pretended not to be staring at them.

'Actually,' Faith said, turning away so most people couldn't see her face, 'why don't we take this conversation out onto the balcony, Lord Beresford? Fewer witnesses that way.'

Sylvia's eyes grew wider still, but Dominic just gave a sharp nod and took her arm. 'Let's go.'

CHAPTER FOURTEEN

Witnesses. She was worried about witnesses. Dominic supposed that he should be grateful she wanted to take the conversation out of the public domain, but instead all he could think about was what on earth she had planned she didn't want witnesses for.

Or perhaps she was more afraid of what he might do. His list of questions rose up in the back of his mind but, in the end, the moment the balcony door swung shut, the first thing he said was simply, 'Why?'

Leaning back against the balcony rails, too high up above ground for Dominic to really feel comfortable with her lounging over them, Faith raised an eyebrow. 'Why what? Why did I leave? Why did I lie? Why am I here?'

'Yes,' he said. He wanted answers to all of them. He also wanted to know how he could be so furious with her and yet so desperate to kiss her at the same time, but he suspected she wouldn't have the answer for that one.

Besides, fury was winning by a comfortable margin.

'You ran away,' he said, the words hard in his mouth. 'I was going to fix this. I could have stopped all of... this.' He waved an arm at the expanse of windows between them and the ballroom, where a host of well-connected people in evening dress were barely even pretending not to be watching them any more. 'All you had to do was stay put and—'

'And let you fix my life?' Faith's voice was cool, colder than he thought he'd heard it before. As if she thought she had some right to be angry with him, after everything that had happened. 'No thank you. My life, my problems, my solutions.'

'Solutions? Since when did running away solve anything?'

Faith tilted her head as she looked at him, and Dominic couldn't tear his eyes away from the lovely line of her neck above her dress. 'That's what this is really about, isn't it? You're mad at me for leaving you.'

His gaze jerked back to her face. 'No! I'm furious because you lied to me. You risked my reputation and you ruined a deal I've been working on for years.'

She stilled, and for a brief moment he thought he saw something like guilt in her face. 'The Americans didn't sign?'

'Not yet. They want to see where we are when things have "settled down".'

Faith winced. 'I'm sorry.'

'*That's* the thing you're sorry for?' He laughed, even though it wasn't funny. 'Of course. The job always meant more to you than I did.'

'No.' Her eyes jumped up to meet his and for a second he almost believed her. 'I'm sorry I couldn't tell you the truth. But I knew how you'd react, what would happen if it got out. I couldn't risk it.'

'Because you needed me. You needed the job.'

'Yes.' Her gaze dropped to her shoes. 'I didn't know who you were either, when I met you. Not when I first asked for the job. And even then...it wasn't until later that I realised what me being, well, me, could do to you. And by then, things between us had become…more.'

Dominic pushed away from the wall and paced across to the edge of the balcony. From there, he could see all over London, all the places he'd never again be able to look at without thinking of her. But it was still better than looking at her face. 'It was never more. The first sign of trouble you ran away, like you always do.'

'I went home.'

'I know.' He shook his head, leaning against the rails as he stared down at the street below. 'Letting me help you was such a terrible prospect that you ran straight to the place you'd been trying to get away from all along.'

'I didn't have a lot of options.' There was an edge in her voice now. Good. She should be angry too. Between them, they'd messed this up good and proper. And even if it was all her fault, he wanted her angry. Wanted her to hate the way their one night had ended.

He shouldn't be the only one being eaten up by the fury.

He couldn't show it anywhere else. To the rest of the world, he needed to be the same in control Lord Beresford he'd always been. This couldn't be seen as more than a tiny blip on his life radar.

But to her…she knew. And so she was the only person he could tear apart.

'You had my credit card,' he pointed out. 'You could have gone anywhere in the world if you'd really wanted.'

Faith gave him a scornful glare. 'You think I'm a common thief, now? Gosh, you really don't have any respect for people outside your social sphere, do you?'

'But you're not outside it. You're Lady Faith.' He spat out the last two words. 'And I've learned a lot about what that means in the last three weeks.'

'Don't believe everything you read in the papers,' she said, as if it were a joke. As if it were even the slightest bit funny.

He turned to face her. He needed to see her reacting to this one. 'Maybe not. But a picture is worth a thousand words, don't they say?'

There. A tremor of something, under the bravado. But still, she tried to excuse herself. 'Like the picture of us?'

'We can't deny what happened just before it, however much we might want to,' he said. 'And it seems like it wasn't your first time in that particular situation.'

That was it. That was the line that got to her. Her whole body, usually so kinetic and full of energy, stopped cold. The only time he'd ever seen her so still was in his hotel room, just before she ran.

Dominic half hoped she might just run again. But she didn't.

'You mean Jared,' Faith said, proud that she could even find her voice. Did he truly think this was the same? That she had some habit of causing scandals for guys and then skipping town?

She'd hoped he knew her better than that. Apparently her real name wasn't the only thing he hadn't realised.

'I heard the poor guy left his wife and kids for you, before you ran. Guess I should be grateful that all I had to lose was my reputation.'

'Funny. I always thought that was all you cared about anyway. If it wasn't, maybe you'd have the wife and kids already and would never have to have worried about me at all.' Ouch, that hurt. It hurt her, and she was the one saying it. But if he honestly believed everything they printed about her...well, a little insult was nothing, surely.

And Dominic wouldn't let her see, even if it did sting. His expression was back to that robot look of the early days, the one that didn't let anything show. The one that had almost convinced her that he wasn't interested in her, didn't want her the way she wanted him.

But she knew better now. She knew him, even if he'd never really known her.

He drew back, leaning away from her against the railings. He wasn't going to rise to the bait. Of course not. As much as she'd love a knock-down drag-out fight with the guy, just to get it all out, to clear the air, maybe even let them start afresh...Dominic would never let go like that. And he'd certainly never do it where they had an audience. Through it all, he'd kept his voice low, his hands clenched at his sides or holding the railings. No outward sign of the fury burning in him.

Well, the crowd behind the glass might not be able to tell, but Faith knew. She knew he was every bit as angry as she was. And she knew he'd never let himself show it.

'So. What are your plans now? Will you stay at Fowlmere as the happy heiress?'

'You mean, will we be required to make polite conversation at every social function until the end of time?' Faith shook her head. 'Thankfully for both of us, no. Dad needs a little help setting up a new project, something to get the estate running properly again, and then I'll be on my way. Fowlmere is only ever a temporary stop for me.'

'You'll be running away again, then. Of course.'

Faith bristled at that. 'I'm not running *from* anything. I'm running *to* something new. My new life. A life where I don't have to answer to people like you.'

He raised an eyebrow. 'People like me?'

'Yes, people like you. And them!' Faith swept an arm out to encompass their audience, just a window pane away. He was the only one on that balcony who cared if they knew they were talking about them. 'All you care about is what other people think about you, what they say. Your precious reputation.'

'What's left of it now you're done with it,' Dominic muttered and grabbed her arm, trying to keep her calm, undemonstrative. Docile.

Ha!

Faith wrenched her arm away. 'Why does it matter to you so much what people think? So your mother left. That's her story, not yours! So you slept with a scandalous runaway heiress. Who cares? And what makes it any of their business anyway?'

'You cared,' he pointed out. 'Or are you trying to tell me that when you ran away the first time it wasn't because of what people were saying about you and Hawkes?' He shook his head. 'All that time I wasted trying to figure out what dreadful secret had made you leave Italy, when all the time I should have been trying to find out why you left Britain in the first place.'

'It wasn't because of Jared,' Faith said, remembering how it had felt, then, to be on the receiving end of that media fever. At least this time she'd actually slept with the guy. 'Not entirely, anyway. I just wanted to be somewhere—someone—else. I wanted people to not care what I did, to be able to live my own life.'

'Without caring what you left behind.'

'That's not true,' she said, but she knew he was never going to understand. 'And you never answered my question. Why does your reputation matter so much to you?'

His lips curved into a cruel smile. 'Didn't you say it yourself? It's all I have.'

'No, it's not.' She looked up at him, willing him to understand this one thing, even if everything else between them would forever be a battleground. 'You have so much more. I saw it, that night in London. The real you. You're more than just Lord Beresford. You're Dominic, too. And you're denying the real you just to keep up a façade in front of people who don't even matter!'

'Whereas you don't even bother with the façade,' he snapped back. 'You just run away when things get hard. You pretend to be anyone except the person you really are. Don't talk to me about denying my true self, *Lady Faith*. I doubt even you know who you really are any more. But it sure as hell isn't this woman in pearls and evening dress.'

Faith's skin burned pink above the fabric of her gown, and Dominic took a perverse pleasure in knowing he could still affect her that way. 'Maybe not. But I know something else I'm not. I'm not going to be your scapegoat any longer. I'm not taking the blame for this. Life is risk. You fail. People leave. And until you take that chance, you'll never be happy. You wanted one night with me, and you got it.'

'And you always told me you were going to leave,' Dominic said. 'At least that was one thing you didn't lie to me about.'

'What, you expected me to stay? As your events coordinator, right? No thanks.'

'I might have wanted more if—'

'If I weren't such a scandal? An embarrassment?'

'That's not it,' he said, but even he knew he was lying.

'Yes. Yes it is.' Faith shook her head and reached for

the balcony door. The buzz and noise of the ballroom filled his ears again as she stepped through. They were talking about them again. It seemed to Dominic they might never stop.

'Goodbye, Dominic,' Faith said, and he had to grip onto the railings to stop himself hauling her back, from making her finish this. He needed her to understand what she'd done to him, what it meant…

He watched as she made her way back into the crowd. Saw her put on her smile, the one that looked completely different to the quick, bright grins he'd seen when she was just Faith Fowler. And nothing at all like the slow, secret smiles she'd given him between kisses, on that last night.

He studied her a little closer. The tension in her shoulders, the slant of her head. The desperation in her eyes. All things he'd never seen before she became Lady Faith again.

She looked as if the walls were closing in on her, bricking her up alive. How hadn't he seen that before? This life, here, was killing her. And he didn't know how to live anything different.

No wonder she'd only ever wanted one night.

'You know,' Sylvia said, sidling up to him, 'that wasn't entirely what I meant when I said "be boring".'

'Faith doesn't know how to be boring,' Dominic said.

'No,' Sylvia agreed, staring out across the ballroom at Lady Faith Fowlmere, too. 'I always liked that about her.'

'Me too,' Dominic admitted.

CHAPTER FIFTEEN

'So. That was an interesting little show you and Lord Beresford put on for us all.' Faith scowled out of the taxi window at her father's words. Bad enough that the whole of London society had been watching through the glass. She didn't need to deconstruct the misery with her father, too.

'It wasn't meant to be for public consumption.' It should have just been her and Dominic, working things out. Making sense of everything that had happened between them. Not just trying to hurt each other without anyone else noticing.

'Wrong venue then, buttercup.' He patted her knee. 'Come on. You know people are fascinated by you. By all of us, really. But especially by you.'

'Maybe that's why I left.'

'And here I thought you didn't care what people thought about you. Wasn't that always what you used to say, when your mother would complain about another photo of you showing your knickers outside a nightclub?' He spoke the words lightly, as always, but Faith thought perhaps there was something harder underneath this time.

'I'm not that girl any more.'

'No, you're not.' Her father smiled at her. 'After all,

you came home this time.' He stretched out his legs as far as the taxi seats would allow and folded his hands behind his head. 'So, are you ready to tell me why you did leave? Really, this time?'

Faith shrugged. 'Nothing complicated. I wanted to be myself, and I felt I couldn't be that with the title round my neck and everyone watching my every screw-up.'

Except Dominic had been right about one thing. She would always be Lady Faith, however much she pretended otherwise. Maybe she really was no better than him. Hiding from her true name wasn't very different from hiding behind a reputation.

'And now?' her dad asked. 'Now you're back. What do you want to be now?'

'Still myself,' Faith replied, because that was always, always going to be true. But… 'Lady Faith, I guess. Whoever she turns out to be.'

'Well, if you really want to find out, seems to me the best place to learn is Fowlmere Manor.'

'I suppose it is.' Could she stay? Should she? Not just for a quick pit stop, but long enough to figure out what it really meant to be Lady Faith Fowlmere, here and now.

'I've got a meeting with Jack tomorrow. We're going to be talking about some of the plans for the estate. You should come with me.'

Was she ready? Getting involved with Dad's scheme…that wasn't something she could just run away from. If she committed to it, she'd have to see it through. Not doing so would mean leaving her parents in the lurch, more than ever before.

Was she ready to take on the responsibility she'd always avoided? Yes, maybe her parents had been responsible for running down the estate. But did that mean she shouldn't help build it back up?

'There'll need to be some changes…' she said.

'I know, I know.' He gave her a self-deprecating smile. 'I know I haven't always done right by you. Or your mother. But we've been trying, you know. When you left…things were bad for a while. But we've turned a corner, I think. And having you home…maybe we can all make it work. Together.'

She'd heard it before, plenty of times. But something in her wanted to believe it was true this time. 'How do I know you won't gamble it away, or get bored and find something better to do?'

'You don't.' He took her hand and squeezed it lightly. 'But, buttercup, what you do know is that it's a lot more likely I'll make a mess of it without you.'

That was true.

Maybe this was something she could do. Something she could be good at.

Maybe, against the odds, the place in the world she'd been searching for, the space she needed to feel at home was, actually, home.

Faith bit her lip. Then she said, 'Give me the guy's number. I'll call and tell him I'm running the project with you now.'

Her father beamed, and Faith hoped she wasn't making a colossal mistake.

'You really should talk to her,' Sylvia said, and Dominic sighed into his paperwork. Was even the office not safe now?

'I can't help but feel we've had this conversation before,' he said, shifting a pile of folders to the middle of his desk, making a wall of filing. 'Don't you have a tea room to run, or something?'

'Russell is taking care of it for the day.' Sylvia

dropped into his client chair and kicked her feet up on his filing wall. 'Which leaves me free to bother you.'

'How wonderful and special.' Dominic reached for the next folder in the stack. He had no idea what it contained, or what he might need it for, but if it meant not talking to Sylvia, he was all for it.

Except she was still sitting there. Watching him. Waiting for him to crack.

'What do I have to do to get rid of you?' he asked.

'Talk to Faith,' she replied promptly.

He sighed and put down the file. 'What on earth could I possibly have to say to her that wasn't already covered, in excruciating public detail, at the event last month?' And in the gossip rags the next day. Everyone was speculating about their mythical on-again, off-again romance. Some even dared to speculate that Faith had spent the last three years in their private love nest on the Continent.

If only they knew the truth, he thought. They'd be so disappointed. Not unlike him.

'That doesn't count,' Sylvia said, which made no sense at all.

'Trust me. It was the most honest conversation we've ever had. Possibly the only honest one.' He shook his head. 'I don't think there's anything left for Faith and I to say to each other.'

'Except that you're in love with her.'

For a moment it seemed so obvious, so profound a truth, that Dominic couldn't speak. Then reality reasserted itself.

'Of course I'm not,' he said, grabbing another handful of files. Where did all these bits of paper even come from? And what happened to them normally, when he wasn't using them to help him ignore his sister?

'Oh, Dominic.' When he looked up, Sylvia was shaking her head sadly. 'Are you really *that* stupid? I mean, I always knew I got the brains in the family. But really?'

'Hey,' he said, a little sharper than he intended.

'Well, right now you are being officially stupid!' Leaning forward to rest her wrists on her knees, Sylvia stared at him so intently he felt obliged to put down the files. 'Listen. She's great. She's honest—fake identity notwithstanding—bright, efficient, gorgeous. She's everything you've ever wanted in a woman.'

'She's a liability,' he countered because he couldn't exactly claim that any of the above weren't true. 'She'd ruin us.' Just like their mother almost had.

'How? By speaking her mind?' Sylvia shook her head. 'You wouldn't want a docile miss who never said what she was really thinking. It would drive you crazy, trying to figure out what she wanted.'

'She's a scandal,' he offered. 'She was caught having an affair with a married man. A drug addict. No one knows where she was for three years. There are all sorts of stories…'

'You know where she was,' Sylvia pointed out. 'Does any of it bother you?'

Yes, Dominic wanted to say. The idea of Faith being with another man, living with him. Loving someone who wasn't him. But he couldn't help but think that might bolster Sylvia's argument more than his own.

Which only left him with the truth.

'She'd leave, Syl. It's what she does.'

Sylvia's face fell, her eyes suddenly very wide. 'Oh, Dominic. You can't possibly think that's true.'

'I don't need to think,' he said, shuffling his files again. 'I know. And she's already done it once! You saw her at the gala last month. She hates that sort of thing.

She hates our whole world. Why else do you think she ran away?'

'But she came back,' Sylvia pointed out. 'She's at Fowlmere right now. It's been weeks and she hasn't left. So maybe she changed her mind?'

He shook his head. If only it were that easy. 'She told me herself, Syl. As soon as she sorts out the mess her father's made of the estate, she's out of there. She'll be back in Florence, or India, or Australia before you can speak. She's not the staying kind.'

'Maybe she just hasn't found something worth staying for yet,' Sylvia suggested in a small, quiet voice.

He gave her a lopsided smile. 'Yeah, well. I think she's made it pretty clear that's not me. Don't you?'

'Faith? It's Sylvia.'

Faith didn't bother asking how Sylvia had got her number—she just assumed she'd stolen it from Dominic's phone. It seemed like a Sylvia thing to do. So, instead, she motioned to Jack to keep walking the hedgerow between the lower and upper fields without her. He knew what they were looking at, and looking for, far better than she did anyway.

'Sylvia. What can I do for you?'

'Oh, I was checking in, see how you're getting on. You're still at the old homestead, I understand?' Sylvia spoke airily, as if it was a matter of no consequence, but Faith knew that if she'd spoken to her brother at all, she had to know that it was.

And yes, she was still at Fowlmere. And, against the odds, actually enjoying being there for the first time she could remember. Which wasn't to say that her parents weren't still capable of driving her crazy at times, but working towards something, as a family, seemed to be making a difference. Even her mother was hard at work pulling out long lost heirlooms and trying to restore them to their possible former glory. Maybe all they'd needed all along was a shared goal.

Maybe that was all she had needed, too.

'I'm still here,' she told Sylvia. 'Actually, it looks like I'll be staying for a while.'

'Helping your father with the estate, I understand?' Faith wondered where she'd heard that. Well, news got around, she supposed. Even when it was a lot more boring than scandalous nights in hotels and missing heiresses.

'Trust me, he needs the help,' she joked.

It was never going to be Beresford, but Faith was discovering that Fowlmere had its own charms, and its own opportunities to shine. To her surprise, she was even excited about them, far more so than planning a tour of some foreign land. This was her home, her heritage, at last. And, for the first time, she wanted to share that with other people.

'So...you think you'll be staying, then?' Sylvia asked.

Suspicion started to prickle at the back of Faith's neck. 'Yeah, it seems like it. Look, Sylvia, not that it's not lovely to hear from you, but was there something that you actually wanted?'

Sylvia sighed down the phone line. 'He's miserable without you.'

'No. He's safe without me. Respectable. Just like he wanted.'

'He was wrong.' Hope tugged at her heart at Sylvia's words, but Faith stamped it back down.

'I can't imagine him saying that.' Or even admitting it to himself.

'Maybe not. But I'm his sister. I know these things. So, you know, bear it in mind.'

Bear it in mind? What did that even mean?

But then a car pulled up on the driveway, just across from the field where she stood, and Faith knew, even before he got out of the car, exactly who the driver was.

CHAPTER SIXTEEN

'BETWEEN YOU AND your sister, this is all starting to feel a little stalkery,' Faith said, folding her arms over her chest as she reached the car.

'My sister?' Dominic asked, cursing Sylvia mentally in his head. This was all her fault, somehow. If it hadn't been for her with her insinuations and questions the day before, he'd never have felt the strange compulsion that led him to check up on Faith. Just to make sure she was okay. And maybe, a little bit, to find out what was making her stay at Fowlmere. 'What did she do?'

'She called. Apparently to check I was still here.'

'And you thought I'd asked her to do that?' Dominic asked.

Faith raised her eyebrows and indicated his presence. 'Not looking entirely far-fetched. Except that I'd have expected it to take you longer to get here.'

'I didn't ask her to call. I imagine she was just concerned for your wellbeing and wanted to see how you are. She's nice like that.' Which sounded much better than, *She's overly invested in our non-existent relationship.*

'Which still doesn't explain what you're doing here.'

'You wouldn't believe the same?' She raised her eyebrows at him. He got the message. 'Fine. I heard you were still here at Fowlmere. And I didn't want to leave things between us as they were. The papers seem to have lost interest, so—'

'So it was safe to come see me. I get it.' There didn't seem much point denying that one.

'I thought maybe you might need some help.' He hadn't been able to get the image of her, confined by evening wear, desperation in her eyes, out of his head. He needed to know she was still here because she wanted to be. Not because she didn't have any other options. 'Word is that you're trying to renovate the Fowlmere estate. Open it for business, like Beresford.'

'I'm not *trying* to do anything. I *am* doing.'

'Right. I just...I didn't expect you to stay this long.' Not voluntarily, anyway.

'You mean you didn't expect me to stay at all.' She looked away, staring out across the fields at some guy with a tape measure. 'Maybe something of what you said stuck. Maybe I'm done with running away.'

'Really.' Stood to reason she wouldn't decide to stay somewhere until *after* she'd run away from him.

'You don't believe me.' She didn't give him time to answer. 'Well, it doesn't matter what you believe. You, or your sister, or the papers, or my parents' friends. I'm back and I'm staying.'

'Why?' Dominic asked, just like he had on the balcony. Would this woman ever stop making him question things?

'Because I found something to stay for,' she said simply, and Dominic stared at the open truth in her face.

She'd found a reason to stay. But it wasn't him. It was never him.

'You were right about one thing,' Faith said. 'Pretending to be someone else, living in hiding, that wasn't being me. I'm Lady Faith Fowlmere, and nothing I do or say will change that. And nobody can take it away from me, either. So I'm here, where I belong. I'm making my own place in the world, not looking for it everywhere else.'

His heart weighed heavy in his chest. He wanted to be happy to see her so free, so alive again. But he couldn't help wish she could have found that happiness with him.

'That's great,' he said. 'And really, I can…I can help. If you want. I've got contacts, been through a lot of the stuff you're going to come up against…'

'Thank you, but no.' She smiled as she spoke, but the words still stung.

'Why not? Because you're too stubborn?'

She shook her head. 'Because I can't have someone in my life who is ashamed of me. I'm done being ashamed of myself. I've made mistakes, sure, but…' She took a breath. 'That's not who I am any more. And I can't have you reminding me at every turn what an embarrassment I am.'

He winced at the reminder. 'When I said…I didn't mean to…'

'Yes. You did.'

'You weren't exactly complimentary to me, either,' he pointed out, and she sighed.

'Look, Dominic, it's okay. Really. We knew each other for, what, a week? It's crazy to think it was anything more than a flirtation. We barely even made it to fling status. It was a one-night stand. Yes, things ended badly, but it's over. You don't have to check up on me, try to help me. You don't even have to feel guilty about the things you said. It's over. We just…move on.'

It was all perfectly reasonable. Almost as if she did

this sort of thing all the time. Rational, even. The sort of sensible argument he'd normally be the one putting forward, not her.

The only problem was, it was a lie.

Whatever had been between them in that week, it was more than a flirtation. More than a fling, even if they never made it past one night together before everything fell apart. And it meant more to him than she could possibly know.

But the most untrue part of all was something he'd been lying to himself about, right up until the moment he saw that tilted chin, the pride in her warm hazel eyes.

He couldn't move on. He needed her in his life. No matter what her past, or who she was. No matter what the papers would say, or his mother's friends, or anyone else.

He needed her. Even more than he wanted her.

Now he just had to convince her of that.

'Dominic?' she asked, and he realised he was staring at her.

'Sorry. Just…thinking.'

She shook her head. 'You think too much. Look, I mean it. You can go.'

He didn't want to. But he needed time. He needed a plan.

Across the field, the burly guy with the tape measure beckoned to her.

'That's Jack,' she said. 'He's helping me with the estate. I've got to go. Thanks, though. For coming and talking to me. It's good to…' she let out a breath '…I don't know. Have closure, maybe.'

'Closure is good,' Dominic agreed. If she wanted to think that this was it, that this was the end for them, fine. It would make it all the more fun to prove her wrong.

Faith bit her lip, then jerked forward suddenly, wrapping her arms around him for a very brief moment. Her body felt stiff, unsure—so unlike the way she'd melted against him in the park at almost midnight, or the way she'd come apart in his arms in bed that night.

A clear sign that this was just not the way it was meant to be.

'Take care of yourself,' she said, stepping back. 'And…I don't know. Try not to overthink things. And loosen up, sometimes, yeah?' She sounded as if she thought she'd never see him again.

'I will,' he promised, watching her walk backwards away from him. His heart hurt just to watch her go, but he held firm. He had to do this properly. He had to find a way to convince her that it didn't matter who she was, where she'd been, what she'd done, or how she might ever embarrass or humiliate him in the future. He loved her. And none of the rest was worth anything, without her.

'Faith?'

She paused. 'Yeah?'

'One more thing. What really happened? With you and that rock star?'

'Jared?' Her eyebrows shot up. 'Didn't you learn everything you needed to about that from the papers?'

He shook his head. 'I don't believe them. You wouldn't do that.'

She bit her lip and he wanted to kiss her, so very badly. 'You're right,' she said. 'It wasn't what it looked like. His wife had just walked out on him, taken the kids, and he'd got himself into a hell of a state at some club. He called me—we were friends, before everything that happened. I picked him up, got him back to his hotel and spent the night sobering him up and listening to him wail about his life. I was taking him home to call his wife and beg her for another chance when they took the photos.' She looked up at him. 'Satisfied?'

'Yes,' he said. He should have known. Should have trusted her. She thought she was a scandal, but really... she was just his Faith. And, for the first time, it didn't matter what anyone else believed about her. 'And thank you. For telling me the truth.'

She shrugged. 'It's a new thing I'm trying. And tell your sister to stop checking up on me, yeah?' Faith added with a grin as she walked away. 'I'm fine.'

Sylvia. She'd help him fix this. Of course she'd also tease and probably hit him, but he could take it.

'Trust me,' he said, smiling at Faith as he climbed back into his car. 'I'm going to go have a long talk with my sister. Right now.'

Faith turned, halfway across the field, and watched his car as it pulled away, trying to ignore the emptiness that threatened to fill her. She'd see him again, she knew. If she was staying at Fowlmere, in society, it was in-evitable. But they'd never be just Dominic and Faith again. She'd never get to take him to see the pelicans or eat at Lola's. She'd never feel his lips against hers, or his body over her.

She'd never get to tell him that she loved him. And she'd given up any chance of ever hearing him say it back.

Loss coursed over her in waves, as if she'd lost her whole life, her whole future, instead of just one man.

It was for the best, she reminded herself, wiping away the tears that dampened her cheeks. She didn't even know if he wanted more—certainly not after everything that had happened. How could she possibly work alongside him, day after day, without giving into the desperate desire for him? And how could she let him help her when she knew he'd be putting his professional and personal reputation on the line to do so?

There was a chance that her plan to save Fowlmere would fail. She wasn't stupid; she knew that. And she couldn't let everything that Dominic had worked for at Beresford be dragged down with it.

Besides, like she'd told him, she was done being ashamed. Done with seeking a place in a world that didn't fit her. She was making her own place, and Dominic Beresford could never understand something like that.

No, this was the perfect ending. A little bittersweet, sure. But they both knew it was the right thing, they had closure, they'd said goodbye.

Now she could move on with her life.

Without the man she loved.

With a shuddering breath, Faith called out to Jack. 'Okay. What's next?'

'You want to do what?' Sylvia screeched to a halt in the middle of the pavement when Dominic announced his intention. He smiled apologetically at the irritated pedestrians who crashed into them.

'Marry Faith,' he said again, his voice calm. It was strange how, once you figured out what needed to be done, the doubt and the worry faded away. All that mattered now was the plan. The right steps he needed to take to make her say yes. 'I'm pretty sure it was your suggestion, actually.'

'I said you were in love with her! I figured you'd date her first. Like a sane person.'

Dominic shook his head. 'It has to be all or nothing.'

'Why?'

'Because she won't say yes to anything else. Actually, she probably won't say yes to this. Which is why I have to get it exactly right.'

Sylvia stared at him, sighed, then started walking again. 'You know, when you said we should go shopping, I was hoping for something more in a shoe line.'

'You don't want to help me choose a ring?'

That changed her mood. 'Yes. Absolutely I do. You're bound to get it wrong without me.'

'So you are in favour of my plan.'

Sylvia lifted a hand and wobbled it from side to side. 'Maybe.'

'How can I convince you?'

Halting in front of the first jewellers shop on the row, Sylvia paused with her finger on the doorbell. 'Tell me why you're doing this.'

Dominic considered. It was one thing to know it was the right move in his head, another to articulate exactly why. Finally, when it became clear they weren't going anywhere until he answered, he said, 'I love her. I'm pretty sure she loves me. I know, in my heart, we belong together.'

'So ask her out. Go for dinner. Take it slow.'

Dominic shook his head. 'Won't cut it. Slow means... it means her worrying I'm going to end things if she does something I find embarrassing. It means leaving an escape route, a way out if she leaves me. A way to pretend it didn't matter. And it means leaving open the chance that we can walk away if things get hard. It means stories and rumours and whispers designed to

try and split us up. And it doesn't show her how I feel.
That it doesn't matter who she is, what she does, any of
it. As long as she's with me. I'll take any risk—even the
risk of her leaving—if she'll give me a chance.'

'A lot of those things can still happen, even if you're
married,' Sylvia pointed out. 'In fact, there'll probably
be more talk if you just rush in like this.'

'I don't care,' Dominic said. 'It won't matter.'

'Because you'll have your ring on her finger.'

'Because she'll be my wife,' Dominic amended.
'Exactly.'

Sylvia rang the bell. 'Then we'd better go choose
you one.'

'Thank you,' Dominic said, grinning. 'For helping.'

'Oh, you're going to need my help with a lot more
than this,' Sylvia said as the jeweller came and opened
the door. 'Have you even thought about how you're
going to propose?'

Dominic smiled. 'Trust me. That part I've got covered.'

CHAPTER SEVENTEEN

IT HAD BEEN a week. One whole long, boring week since they said goodbye. Faith had tried to keep busy, knowing that the only way she was going to get over Dominic was by stopping thinking about him. When she was knee-deep in dusters, polish and tarnished brass, it was harder to remember nights in luxury hotel suites, working together, both watching for a sign of something more...

No. Work was the thing. She couldn't daydream when she was discussing the estate plans with Jack, or working with her parents to clear decades' worth of junk from the attics. Jack had the first round of potential investors visiting at the end of the month—and she had tons of work to do before then.

Work was the way forward. Not worrying about her parents, who seemed a little saner every day. Not thinking about Dominic, who was gone. Not even wondering why Sylvia kept ringing. Faith ignored the calls. She'd moved on. She had closure. No point ruining all that now.

Except it seemed Sylvia wasn't very good at taking a hint.

'Sylvia!' Faith said, hopping down the steps of Fowlmere Manor to meet the car. 'I wasn't expecting you.'

'That's because you don't answer your phone any more. I've come to take you down to town for the day.'

Faith groaned inside. 'That's very kind of you, but I've got a lot on here at the moment…'

'Exactly why you need a day off! Come on, we can go shopping again.'

Faith didn't have especially fond memories of their last shopping trip, but she did like Sylvia and she really didn't want to hurt her feelings. Besides, she did need a new suit for the investors meeting…

'I've got Dominic's credit card,' Sylvia said, waving the card temptingly.

'I don't need that.' Faith was pretty sure there was a little bit of room left on her own.

'Just jump in,' Sylvia urged, and Faith gave up the fight.

'Okay. Let me just settle up a few things here…'

With hindsight, she should have been more suspicious from the start. If not then, certainly when Sylvia drove them straight to the Greyfriars Hotel for their lunch. But Sylvia kept chatting about nothing and keeping everything light and unimportant, so Faith's suspicions only really started to grow when they stepped outside at the exact same moment a red double-decker tour bus pulled up.

'What fun! A tour!' Even Sylvia didn't manage to not sound fake at that one.

'What's going on?' Faith said, rounding on Dominic's sister.

'I've always wanted to take a London bus tour,' Sylvia said, obviously lying. 'Come on, you can be my tour guide! You can stand up front with the microphone and everything.'

'They normally hire someone in to do that,' Faith

said as Sylvia dragged her up the bus steps and grabbed the microphone from its stand, handing it to her. 'Besides, it's been years since I did a bus tour. I've probably forgotten everything…'

She trailed off. She wasn't suspicious any more. Because she knew beyond a shadow of a doubt that she'd been set up.

Lord Dominic Beresford sat in the bus driver's seat.

'What are you—' The words echoed around the bus and she fumbled for the off switch on the microphone. 'What are you doing here?' she whispered.

Dominic grinned at her. 'Sylvia's always wanted to take one of these tours. So I commandeered a tour bus. We figured you could do the guide bit for old times' sake.' As if that were the most normal thing in the world.

Faith glanced back. A bus full of tourists stared at her, cameras and guidebooks at the ready. 'For the love of… You stole a tour bus? You? Lord Beresford?'

'Borrowed,' Dominic corrected. Starting the engine, he checked his mirrors and put the bus in gear. 'You remember that night you showed me your London?'

As if she could ever forget. 'Yes.'

'Well, today I'm going to show you mine.' The bus pulled away from the kerb. 'Come on, tour guide, aren't you supposed to be talking into that thing?'

Faith stared at the microphone in her hand. 'I don't know where we're going.'

'Yes you do,' Dominic said, and started to drive.

Dominic wiped the palm of his hand against his trousers before grabbing the steering wheel again. In his pocket, the hard lump of the ring box dug into him, a sharp-edged reminder of exactly what craziness he was pursuing. Oh, not the proposal, exactly. That, he was certain about. But the method... How had he thought this was a good idea?

Maybe it wasn't. But it was the only chance he had of convincing Faith he was serious. If nothing else, she couldn't worry about his fear of embarrassment any longer. Nothing she could ever do could humiliate him more than what he was about to do. Especially since he suspected his sister would be secretly filming the whole thing to share with the Internet.

Beside him, Faith had begun her tour, talking in only a slightly wobbly voice about the landmarks they passed. He'd decided to start off with the usual tour route, down past St Paul's and Fleet Street before he detoured over the river after the Tower of London. Faith still knew this route backwards, she'd told him on their tour of her London, and, for now, he was happy to let her talk, feel comfortable. As if this really was an official tour with an unusual driver.

'The Tower of London has a long and varied history,' Faith said, and Dominic risked a glance out of his window at the landmark. Maybe he'd take her there one day, just to listen to her get excited about the stories the building could tell. 'Most notably, of course, it's known as the site of the murder of the princes in the tower...'

Not romantic enough, Dominic decided. Time to start the plan properly.

Swinging the bus over to the other lane, he headed for the bridge over the Thames, ignoring Faith's murmured protest. Then, as they crossed over the water, she put her hand over the microphone. 'You're going the wrong way.'

'I'm really not.'

'They usually go along to Big Ben and the Houses of Parliament next,' she argued.

Dominic flashed her a smile. 'Trust me. I know exactly where we're going. Now, give me the microphone.'

'What?' She grabbed it closer to her chest at his request.

'Put it on the stand there so I can talk into it,' he said, nodding towards the steering wheel.

'What are you going to say?' she asked, but she did install the microphone as he'd asked.

'I'm not a hundred per cent sure yet,' Dominic admitted. 'But I'm sure I'll figure it out as I go along.'

Figure it out as he went along. Faith was pretty sure Dominic had never figured out anything as he went along. The man liked to have a plan. A fixed, unchanging, reputation-saving plan. So what on earth was he doing?

Sinking down into the guide's chair at the front of the bus, hands gripping the arm rests too tightly, she waited to find out.

'Hello, everyone. I'm your driver, Dominic. I'm afraid that today's tour is going to be taking a little bit of a detour. You see, not very long ago, your tour guide, Faith, introduced me to a side of London—and a side of myself—I'd never seen before. Then, for reasons we really don't need to get into, but suffice to say it was mostly my fault, she left me here alone in this big city. And now I want to show her my London, and how it looks without her.'

Faith's cheeks burned at his words. She couldn't look at him, couldn't even acknowledge what he was saying. Was he trying to humiliate her? Was this some sort of ridiculous revenge? No. This was Dominic. Whatever

might have happened between them, he wouldn't do
that to her.

'And, Faith?' he said. 'Trust me, this is going to be
far more embarrassing for me than it is for you.'

Somehow, she wasn't entirely convinced.

'On your right, you can just about still see the River
Thames.' Dominic's voice automatically took on the ca-
dence she'd heard when he was presenting at meetings,
or holding court over debate at the dinner table. 'We're
now officially on the South Bank. Coming up, you'll see
the back of Shakespeare's Globe Theatre, amongst other
things. We can't really get close enough to the river in
this big old thing, but that's okay. All you really need to
know is that every single time I walk along this river, I
think about Faith. I remember walking along the South
Bank with her, practically in the middle of the night,
looking out over the London skyline.'

Faith was pretty sure that wasn't all he remembered.
Whenever she thought of it, her body remembered his
arms around her, his chest under her cheek, the way he'd
kissed her as if she were the air he needed to breathe...

'As we swing around here,' Dominic said as the bus
lurched around the corner, 'we can head back over the
river. From here you can see the London Eye, and across
the way the Houses of Parliament. But what really matters is, if you look back along the river the way we came,
you can see Tower Bridge in the sunshine.'

Tower Bridge. The place they'd first had dinner with
all his clients. What on earth did he remember about
that night? Behind her, the tour group were all whispering, chatting and giggling. About her, Faith assumed.
Well, at least they were having fun. And it wasn't as if
she hadn't had more embarrassing moments in her life.
Even if she wasn't exactly sure what this one was lead-

ing up to. Another way to convince her to let him help with Fowlmere? A really weird first date?

'Tower Bridge was where I first realised how incredibly smart, intelligent, organised and good at her job Faith is. How she could take on my job in a second if she wanted. Anything she sets her mind to, this woman can do.'

Faith tilted her head to stare at the ceiling, trying to ignore the blush burning her cheeks.

'Is it working, love?' the old woman sitting behind her asked. 'Have you forgiven him?'

'It's not about forgiveness,' Faith muttered, sitting up straight again. 'We agreed this was a bad idea, is all. I'm not going to work with him.'

'I don't think that's what he's asking, dear,' the woman said. 'Besides, I don't think he's finished yet.'

As Dominic steered the bus back across the river, he pointed out the spot where they first kissed, giving her a lingering look as he spoke that nearly resulted in them crashing into a bollard.

'Eyes on the road,' Faith screeched.

Dominic laughed and, before they'd gone very much further, pulled into a bus stop and pulled on the brake. 'Okay, ladies and gentlemen. This is where we need to continue our tour on foot, I'm afraid.'

'Dominic!' Faith said, even as the tourists started gathering their bags and cameras. 'These people have paid for a bus tour, not a walking tour. That's what they expect.'

'They'll like this more,' Dominic promised her, planting a swift kiss on her lips. 'And I hope you will too. Come on!'

She couldn't help but jump down off the bus after

him, her lips still tingling from his kiss. But then she stopped on the pavement.

'Wait. Just… Dominic. Wait.'

Twenty paces up ahead, at the front of the gaggle of tourists in their cagoules, cameras at the ready, Dominic stopped, turned and looked at her.

'I just…I don't understand what's going on. I don't know what you want.' Tears burned at the back of her eyes, and Faith blinked them away. 'Why are you doing this? We agreed…'

'We were wrong.' Dominic walked back towards her, and held out his hand. 'We were stupid to think we could just put this away in a box and ignore it. I'm never going to be able to walk through St James's Park without thinking of you. Without wanting you in my life. It's not possible.'

A small, sharp flare of hope burst into life in her chest. 'So, you want…'

'I want you to come with me to see the pelicans,' Dominic said.

'Okay.' Faith nodded. She could do that.

CHAPTER EIGHTEEN

GETTING THE WHOLE group of them across the road and into the park was quite an operation. Dominic would happily have left them to find their own way there—they all knew their jobs, after all—but Faith was in full tour guide mode again, shepherding them all across and stopping traffic just by standing in the middle of the road. It made Dominic's heart clench just to watch.

But finally they were all through the gates of St James's Park and the last, most important part of the plan was in motion. Maybe the first part hadn't gone quite as well as he'd intended when he'd described his plans to Sylvia; her storyboard for the afternoon—which Dominic fully intended to frame and give to Faith on their first anniversary—had included Faith swooning into his lap with delight before he'd even started driving.

This part, though, he had faith in. How could she resist pelicans, the perfect ring, and the most romantic, embarrassing proposal of all time?

This was weird. This was officially the weirdest thing any man had ever done for her. And she still wasn't entirely sure what exactly was going on. All she knew was that she was walking around St James's Park with

the man she loved, and fifty total strangers, looking
for pelicans.

Totally normal.

'There's one!' one of the tourists yelled out, and suddenly everyone was crowded around the edge of the
lake, staring at it. Faith hung back, Dominic beside
her, and watched. Then, without warning or any obvious sign, the whole group turned back to face them,
grinning manically.

'What's going—' Faith started, then stopped as she
heard music. Impossible, lilting music coming from
some sort of sound system somewhere. She looked
around, trying to spot where it was coming from, to
figure out what everyone was looking at—

'It had to be you,' Dominic sang, his voice strong
and sure and only slightly off-key.

Faith froze, even as he smiled at her. And then he
started to dance. Faith clapped a hand to her mouth
as Dominic foxtrotted around her with an imaginary
partner as he sang. It was, by far, the most surreal moment of her life.

Around her, the tour group picked up the tune to
the classic song and supported Dominic as he dropped
to one knee. And then, like some sort of crazy dream,
they started to move, stepping in perfect unison to the
side, then into pairs, clearly rehearsed and planned and
anticipated by everyone who wasn't her.

Their dance, choreographed to the last step, swirled
around them, the words coming clean and strong in
sopranos, altos, tenors and basses. Faith blinked with
disbelief, even as she watched. Crowds were forming
on the paths beyond, staring as the bus of people she'd
tried to tell about the Tower of London foxtrotted in
perfect time through the park, singing as they went.

Bystanders were joining in now, and right by the lake Faith spotted Sylvia, hand to her mouth with excitement. Even the pelicans seemed to be enjoying themselves.

And there, at her feet, was Dominic, holding out a ring box.

'Too much?' he asked.

'Um...'

'Only I wanted you to know. You're worth any embarrassment. Any story in any paper. I can ignore any of it if I have you with me.' He sounded so earnest, so open. Faith couldn't remember ever seeing him like that, except in this place. And one precious night when he'd let himself go, only to have everything ruined.

'Even if I'm a scandal?' Because she was. And probably always would be. If he wanted her, he had to want all of her, even the parts that were too brash, or showed off too much cleavage, or walked up to strangers in airport bars and demanded a job.

'I don't care,' he said, so swiftly she couldn't help but believe him.

'I suppose no one is going to ever find anything to laugh at you for more than this,' Faith mused as the performers reached the climax of the song.

'Unless you say no,' Dominic pointed out.

'I should, you know,' Faith said. 'Just to be sure you can really take the humiliation.'

Dominic flipped open the ring box, letting the sunshine sparkle off a diamond that could probably fix the roof of the west wing at Fowlmere. 'Are you going to?'

Faith looked down at him, into his warm eyes, his raised eyebrow, and thought, *How I love this man.* He was, by turn, ridiculously stiff and unyielding, then hilariously open and embarrassing. She might never get a handle on him completely. On how to make him open up when he needed to, and how to know when something was too much.

She'd probably embarrass him a thousand times over, and he'd probably drive her crazy at least once a day. The society pages would talk of nothing else for weeks. He'd want to interfere in everything she did at Fowlmere, then forget to ask her advice at Beresford.

But they'd sneak off to Lola's once a month, and book a suite at the Greyfriars when they needed to get away from it all. She'd get to be herself, not Lady Faith, not Faith Fowler, just her. Because she knew, beyond anything else, that was who he loved most.

There was a lot they'd need to figure out. But they'd get there. She had faith.

'You're not afraid I'll run away?'

He shook his head. 'I'll take the chance. Besides, I don't care where you go, as long as you always come back to me.'

The song finished and the dancers crowded round them, panting slightly, not adding anything at all to the romance.

'So. What's your answer? Are you going to say no to test my humiliation level?'

'Yes,' Faith said.

Dominic's brow crumpled. 'Yes, you're going to say no? Or yes, you'll marry me?'

Faith laughed, her hair blowing in the breeze, and reached down a hand to pull him to his feet. 'Yes, I'll marry you. Even though you hijacked a bus and proposed to me by flash mob.'

His arms were around her waist in less than a second, before the crowd even started cheering.

'It was the only way I could think of to convince you,' he murmured as he leant in to kiss her.

'Well, it worked,' Faith said, stretching up on tiptoe. 'Remind me not to let you search for wedding speeches on the Internet?'

'Will do.' And then he kissed her and she forgot her sister-in-law-to-be, filming everything from the side, forgot the flash mob, forgot the crowds; she even forgot the pelicans.

She only knew she'd never need to run away again.

* * * * *

Mills & Boon® Hardback
February 2014

ROMANCE

A Bargain with the Enemy	Carole Mortimer
A Secret Until Now	Kim Lawrence
Shamed in the Sands	Sharon Kendrick
Seduction Never Lies	Sara Craven
When Falcone's World Stops Turning	Abby Green
Securing the Greek's Legacy	Julia James
An Exquisite Challenge	Jennifer Hayward
A Debt Paid in Passion	Dani Collins
The Last Guy She Should Call	Joss Wood
No Time Like Mardi Gras	Kimberly Lang
Daring to Trust the Boss	Susan Meier
Rescued by the Millionaire	Cara Colter
Heiress on the Run	Sophie Pembroke
The Summer They Never Forgot	Kandy Shepherd
Trouble On Her Doorstep	Nina Harrington
Romance For Cynics	Nicola Marsh
Melting the Ice Queen's Heart	Amy Ruttan
Resisting Her Ex's Touch	Amber McKenzie

MEDICAL

Tempted by Dr Morales	Carol Marinelli
The Accidental Romeo	Carol Marinelli
The Honourable Army Doc	Emily Forbes
A Doctor to Remember	Joanna Neil

Mills & Boon® Large Print
February 2014

ROMANCE

The Greek's Marriage Bargain	Sharon Kendrick
An Enticing Debt to Pay	Annie West
The Playboy of Puerto Banús	Carol Marinelli
Marriage Made of Secrets	Maya Blake
Never Underestimate a Caffarelli	Melanie Milburne
The Divorce Party	Jennifer Hayward
A Hint of Scandal	Tara Pammi
Single Dad's Christmas Miracle	Susan Meier
Snowbound with the Soldier	Jennifer Faye
The Redemption of Rico D'Angelo	Michelle Douglas
Blame It on the Champagne	Nina Harrington

HISTORICAL

A Date with Dishonour	Mary Brendan
The Master of Stonegrave Hall	Helen Dickson
Engagement of Convenience	Georgie Lee
Defiant in the Viking's Bed	Joanna Fulford
The Adventurer's Bride	June Francis

MEDICAL

Miracle on Kaimotu Island	Marion Lennox
Always the Hero	Alison Roberts
The Maverick Doctor and Miss Prim	Scarlet Wilson
About That Night...	Scarlet Wilson
Daring to Date Dr Celebrity	Emily Forbes
Resisting the New Doc In Town	Lucy Clark

Mills & Boon® Hardback
March 2014

ROMANCE

A Prize Beyond Jewels	Carole Mortimer
A Queen for the Taking?	Kate Hewitt
Pretender to the Throne	Maisey Yates
An Exception to His Rule	Lindsay Armstrong
The Sheikh's Last Seduction	Jennie Lucas
Enthralled by Moretti	Cathy Williams
The Woman Sent to Tame Him	Victoria Parker
What a Sicilian Husband Wants	Michelle Smart
Waking Up Pregnant	Mira Lyn Kelly
Holiday with a Stranger	Christy McKellen
The Returning Hero	Soraya Lane
Road Trip With the Eligible Bachelor	Michelle Douglas
Safe in the Tycoon's Arms	Jennifer Faye
Awakened By His Touch	Nikki Logan
The Plus-One Agreement	Charlotte Phillips
For His Eyes Only	Liz Fielding
Uncovering Her Secrets	Amalie Berlin
Unlocking the Doctor's Heart	Susanne Hampton

MEDICAL

Waves of Temptation	Marion Lennox
Risk of a Lifetime	Caroline Anderson
To Play with Fire	Tina Beckett
The Dangers of Dating Dr Carvalho	Tina Beckett

Mills & Boon® Large Print
March 2014

ROMANCE

Million Dollar Christmas Proposal	Lucy Monroe
A Dangerous Solace	Lucy Ellis
The Consequences of That Night	Jennie Lucas
Secrets of a Powerful Man	Chantelle Shaw
Never Gamble with a Caffarelli	Melanie Milburne
Visconti's Forgotten Heir	Elizabeth Power
A Touch of Temptation	Tara Pammi
A Little Bit of Holiday Magic	Melissa McClone
A Cadence Creek Christmas	Donna Alward
His Until Midnight	Nikki Logan
The One She Was Warned About	Shoma Narayanan

HISTORICAL

Rumours that Ruined a Lady	Marguerite Kaye
The Major's Guarded Heart	Isabelle Goddard
Highland Heiress	Margaret Moore
Paying the Viking's Price	Michelle Styles
The Highlander's Dangerous Temptation	Terri Brisbin

MEDICAL

The Wife He Never Forgot	Anne Fraser
The Lone Wolf's Craving	Tina Beckett
Sheltered by Her Top-Notch Boss	Joanna Neil
Re-awakening His Shy Nurse	Annie Claydon
A Child to Heal Their Hearts	Dianne Drake
Safe in His Hands	Amy Ruttan

0214 GEN STD LP

Discover more romance at

www.millsandboon.co.uk

- ❤ WIN great prizes in our exclusive competitions

- ❤ BUY new titles before they hit the shops

- ❤ BROWSE new books and REVIEW your favourites

- ❤ SAVE on new books with the Mills & Boon® Bookclub™

- ❤ DISCOVER new authors

PLUS, to chat about your favourite reads, get the latest news and find special offers:

- Find us on facebook.com/millsandboon
- Follow us on twitter.com/millsandboonuk
- Sign up to our newsletter at millsandboon.co.uk